Fallen Angel

G. L. BURN

ISBN: 978-1-52015-696-5

DEDICATION

To Terry. You're my role model, my biggest fan and
my best friend. Thank you for believing in me.

CONTENTS

CHAPTER 1

"What did Sir Adrian tell you about this business?" Adolfo Oscar, first rank demon and Head of Station H, leaned back in his elegant S-bend leather and chrome chair and stared out of the window of his office.

Third rank demon Victor Bischoff followed the direction of his gaze, watching the thick flurries of snow with a sense of dismay. Helsinki railway station crouched on the other side of the road, the grey stone giants on the facade frozen beneath a layer of ice. Victor hadn't seen weather like this for years. Oxford had been cold and damp, but Helsinki was different: a dry freeze that made his bones ache. Never mind that he was half Finnish; the fabled sisu seemed to be completely absent from his DNA. A draught crept into the room, stirring the surface of his coffee, and he lifted the cup before the drink could lose its warmth.

"He told me nothing." Victor took a sip and almost moaned in delight at the heady caffeine rush. The complex legislation governing the import of coffee, a Grade One narcotic for demons, meant that even the 'safe' decaffeinated blends intended for human consumption were a rare and expensive treat in England. After months of drinking sweetened ground chicory, he'd almost forgotten the ecstasy of real coffee. Victor took another appreciative sip before he continued, "Sir Adrian thought I was being seconded to Station H's Field Unit."

"Hmm." Adolfo swung around in his chair and fixed Victor with a curious, watchful gaze. "Technically that's correct. London Central telexed your file over this morning. Quite the clever lad, aren't we?"

Victor sensed the question was rhetorical and stayed quiet.

"London seems to think you have some ability with interrogation. Ah, here we are." Adolfo plucked a buff-coloured file from a wobbling stack of papers and opened it, flicking through the foolscap pages until he came to a stop. "Your tours of duty in the south of France have been commended twice. Likewise, the Head of Station V lauded your work with a group of Italian refugees."

Silence. Victor glanced down at his almost empty cup and then looked with longing at the steel-brushed coffee pot on the sideboard. "Thank you, sir."

Adolfo dropped the file back onto his desk and steepled his hands, his gaze intent. "We find ourselves with an unprecedented situation."

Alert to his tone of voice, Victor sat up straight. "What kind of situation?"

Adolfo swung his chair around and resumed looking out of the window. "I take it you watched the most recent telecast."

"I did, but it was broadcast in Finnish."

"Yes, of course. You really should learn the language." Adolfo seemed annoyed, as if it was a personal affront. "Channel 32 for German, 38 for English, for future reference."

Victor balanced the coffee cup on his knee. "I gather some kind of meteor fell to the ground outside Hamënlinna."

"It wasn't a meteor."

Keeping his face impassive, Victor nodded. "A missile of some sort?" He hoped not. Such crude weapons had been banned and dismantled following World War Three, when angels and demons had intervened to stop humankind from destroying the earth. There were always rumours of new technologies in far-flung countries and the threat of a dirty bomb, but Victor hadn't heard anything in his most recent tour to Austria, and there'd been nothing on the tickers in his Oxford workplace, an encryption/monitoring station for worldwide contact strings.

"Not a missile, either." Adolfo gave him a crooked smile. "It was an angel."

The cup almost tipped over into his lap. Victor righted it, his pulse quickening and a frisson of anticipation going through him. "An angel? A real one?" He caught himself, curbing his enthusiasm as he realised he must sound stupid. A blush burned his cheeks, and he covered it by taking another sip of coffee.

Adolfo picked up his own drink and dunked a small biscuit into the coffee. "Have you ever seen an angel before, Officer Bischoff?"

"Not a live one." Victor tried to suppress his excitement. "The only angel I've seen was the plasticised exhibit that toured the Trade Manifold countries ten years ago. My dad took me to see it."

"Ah, yes. I heard about it but never saw it. I remember the telecasts discussing the ethics of it. The humans were fascinated, of course—they're always fascinated by angels. And the nature of the exhibit—a dead angel injected with plastic to preserve its looks, right down to the finest downy feather. Was it Art? Was it Science? The usual rubbish spouted by ethical moralists..." Adolfo ate the soggy biscuit and returned his gaze to Victor. "What did you think of it?"

Wondering if this was some sort of test, Victor decided upon a careful answer. "The wings were beautiful."

Adolfo snorted. "Wings. That's all anyone's ever interested in." He set down his coffee and stood, leaning forward across his desk as his pale silvery wings unfurled. The membranes between each joint appeared tissue-thin, tattered in places and marked all over with scars.

Victor drew in a soft breath. Demon wings were nowhere near as aesthetically pleasing as angel wings, and unlike their heavenly cousins, demons couldn't regenerate damaged wings. Scars and rips stayed part of the body forever. Wing repair and healing was a costly and complicated business with only a small percentage of success. Within the countries of the Demon Trade Manifold, or DTM, it was considered fortunate by human surgeons working for the demon-controlled government that only demons of second rank and above could grow wings.

Adolfo's wings were damaged badly enough that Victor could tell he'd never fly again. He remembered the old rumour that Adolfo had been involved in a torrid inter-departmental clash with the Controller of the German Desk, Jeremy Wiedemann. Victor had seen Wiedemann on several occasions, his first rank wings glittering with bright scarlet tips. When he'd been much younger, he'd wanted to have wings like that when he grew up.

"It's useful to know your enemy, sir," Victor

offered. "The angels, I mean."

"Is that how you see them? Enemies?" Adolfo looked annoyed, his wings flicking back and settling into their tight, folded shape. "What the Hell do they teach you in training school these days?"

Swallowing a flash of anxiety, Victor fell back on a textbook reply. "I know how to interrogate and rehabilitate citizens from the Federation Internationale d'Anges. I know the rights of humankind in both the DTM and the FIA, and our responsibilities to them, and theirs to us, their saviours and governors. I studied the history of the conflict created by World War Three and the ensuing battle between demons and angels and the social implications it caused. I came top of my class in—"

Adolfo made an irritated gesture. "I'm not interested in all that. I've read your dossier. What I want to know is how you view the angels. Tell me honestly, without the bullshit."

"Honestly?" Victor thought for a moment, his mind overflowing with information he'd been taught all his life. He knew so much about angels, most of it contradictory, and yet he'd never been able to draw any solid conclusions. "I don't know, sir. I always thought I'd be able to form an opinion once I'd met one."

"All that education and you don't know." Adolfo gave a small smile as he retrieved his cup and crossed the room to the sideboard. "Do you fear them?"

"No."

"You should. Don't trust an angel. They're devious creatures." Lifting the coffee pot, Adolfo swirled its contents as if to judge how much was left. He poured a thick, scented stream of the black liquid into his cup before adding cream and sugar. "My most promising field officer was seduced by an angel. It caused a terrible scandal."

Victor held out his cup with alacrity when Adolfo approached with the pot. "I don't remember any scandal, sir."

"It was covered up at the highest level." Adolfo returned the empty pot to the sideboard and sat back down again behind his desk. "Officer Bertram was in line for promotion. He could have gone right to the top—perhaps he'd have become Controller of the Scandinavian Desk within a few years. Instead he threw it all away when he got involved with a Spanish angel, Raul Soler."

"How did they meet? Was Soler trying to defect?" It happened occasionally—a demon ran into the FIA or an angel crossed into the DTM, but such occurrences were rare and usually highly publicized to cause maximum embarrassment to the other side. Victor couldn't remember anything like this happening since he was a child.

Adolfo drained his cup and replaced it in its saucer with a bang. "Bertram was in Switzerland investigating a financial issue. Soler got to him. Seduced him. He claims he wasn't working under orders from the FIA, but I'm sure he was. Isaac didn't stand a chance. They both lost their wings over it, and now they're stuck in Switzerland."

Victor almost choked on his mouthful of coffee. A demon giving up his wings wasn't something to be taken lightly. In effect, it made him mortal, limiting his power and lifespan to that of an average human. It was irreversible and, according to his father, who claimed to have seen it done, the spell to remove the wings caused extreme agony.

"Officer Bertram must have cared for the angel very much," he mumbled into his cup. "And vice versa."

Adolfo snorted. "He's a fool. So much promise gone to waste. But you..." He jabbed a finger at him. "Officer Bischoff, you must be vigilant. Be on your guard when you conduct your interrogations. You must always be one step ahead. This case is vitally important."

A warm glow of pride wrapped around him. Victor beamed. "I will do my best. Thank you, sir."

Adolfo delved into the pile of paperwork on his desk again and picked up a dark grey folder fixed shut with wax seals and tied with crimson ribbons. "This is everything we know about our fallen angel. You can read it on the way to the interrogation unit in Turku. In this weather it'll take you a couple of hours to get up there. It's not luxury accommodation, I'm afraid, but then it's not meant to be the Ritz. Officer Olsen will meet you and be your point of contact. Ask him anything. I'll expect a preliminary report at the end of the week."

"Yes, sir." Victor finished his coffee, draining it to the gritty dregs.

Adolfo seemed amused by his actions. "I keep forgetting Britain allows only a limited import of coffee."

"It was British scientists who discovered the long-term effects of high grade coffee on demons," Victor reminded him. A dribble of coffee remained in the bowl of the teaspoon. He picked it up and licked away the last trace of the liquid, feeling the caffeine sing through him.

"In Finland, we allow demons to be sensible with their coffee intake," Adolfo said, still amused. "Those who wish to overindulge, go insane, and die painful deaths may do so with our blessing."

"I prefer to trust in the regulatory sanctions imposed by the British government."

Adolfo chuckled. "That's why Britain has a terrible problem with black market coffee. Not all buyers are demons, of course, but..."

"It's the fastest-growing crime in the country." The taste of the coffee lingered on Victor's tongue, souring slightly as the hit from the caffeine started to fade. "No one knows where the illegal imports are coming from."

Adolfo waved the beribboned folder. "From the angels, of course. That's why this case is so important. Our fallen angel could provide enough evidence to break several smuggling rings all across the DTM. Britain isn't the only country suffering from high profile black market smuggling. Break this angel, and we could blow this business wide open."

Victor stood and collected the dossier. "How do you know that..." he paused to read the name typewritten on the front of the folder, "Ruben Patrick Barbosa is involved in any of this business?"

Raising his eyebrows, Adolfo gave him a droll look. "His father owns the largest coffee plantations in Brazil, has a dozen blending and manufacturing plants in FIA territory, and controls a sixty-four percent market share of the entire industry."

Victor wanted to kick himself. He'd only been on the job for an hour and he'd already managed to ask the type of question made by callow recruits straight out of training college. This was his big chance to prove himself, to step out from his father's shadow and show his worth as a DTM operative. He couldn't afford to make any mistakes. Clutching the folder, he said fervently, "I won't let you down, sir."

Adolfo nodded. "I'm sure you'll do everything the situation demands."

Victor tucked the folder under his arm, adjusted the angle, and strode across the office. At the door, he turned as a sudden thought came to him. "Sir, Station H has trained interrogators. Why use me?"

Adolfo smiled, but it didn't reach his eyes. "Why not?"

CHAPTER 2

Victor paused in front of Room 22 and checked he had everything he needed to conduct the interrogation. Dossier, police reports, paper, pencils. He drew in a quivering breath then released it on a sigh. He had no reason to be nervous. He'd conducted dozens of interviews, some much more comprehensive and difficult than this. So his subject was an angel this time. Big deal. Whatever. So not important.

He scrunched his eyes shut. For a demon, he was a bad liar. He couldn't even lie convincingly to himself.

A sound behind him made him turn. Emil Olsen, the officer who ran the Turku safe house/interrogation unit, made a shooing motion. Victor resisted making a gesture in return and faced the door again. Another deep breath and he strode forward, flicked the lock, and entered the room.

After the darkness of the corridor, the light pouring into the interrogation room startled him. The white-painted walls seemed to shine, the brightness coming from the snow-coated landscape and the brutal paleness of the grey sky visible through the large sash window. In vivid contrast, the furniture was dark, cheap, and tatty. A small two-bar heater glowed orange on the paint-spattered floorboards.

Victor took in the decor with a sense of dismay. His training kicked in, reminding him of Article 67 in the departmental guidelines: Make a joke about the surroundings, imply you can upgrade the subject to better accommodation, and they'll be inclined to trust you. He opened his mouth to make an appropriate remark, and then every rational thought flew out of his head as he faced the subject.

Ruben Patrick Barbosa grinned at him. "Hello, buttercup."

His carefully gathered papers almost dropped to the floor. Victor stood in the doorway, frozen for a moment as he tried to reconcile what he'd studied with what he saw in the middle of the room.

Ruben lounged in a hard wooden chair, one bare foot curled over the edge of the heavy oak table in front of him. The chair was tilted on its back legs, and Ruben rocked to and fro. He wore a pair of tight, pale blue denim jeans and nothing else.

Victor stared, his mind in freefall. He knew he should look away—he'd seen half-naked men before, after all—but somehow none of the others had been quite as glorious as this. Smooth, tawny-honey skin. An agreeably muscled torso. A dark, soft stripe of body hair. A breathtakingly handsome face with a faint scar on his left cheek, heavy eyebrows under an artfully disheveled mop of shiny black hair, and a curious, guarded expression in those bitter-chocolate eyes.

Something was wrong. Victor cursed his luck, wondering why Station H hadn't seen fit to append a photograph of Ruben Patrick Barbosa to his dossier. His brain hammered at him—something is missing—but lust roiled around, distracting him from his job. Victor kept staring, feeling the blush rise to his face and heat spread through his body as he gazed at the half-naked angel sprawled in front of him.

Angel. That was it. Wings!

Victor dragged in a breath and lifted his chin. Annoyance filled him, displacing the lust. His father had warned him that something like this would happen at least once in his career. Valdemar Bischoff had been the Monaco Resident for almost twenty years, an unheard-of period of time to hold such a position. Though a senior official within the DTM government, it was whispered that Valdemar had angered the Director-General, the Deputy, and just about every Controller of every European desk. By rights, Valdemar should have moved into one of the Controller jobs ten years ago. Instead, he was stuck in the dangerous backwater of Monaco.

Valdemar never spoke of the past, and Victor respected his father too much to ask. He knew it would be tough to prove his own worth while carrying the baggage of his father's actions, but so far his rise through the ranks of the service had been painless. Now it seemed he was being tested. Two of the most basic pieces of information had been left out of the dossier: Not only was Ruben Patrick Barbosa as beautiful as sin, he was also missing his wings.

Victor set down the papers and pencils on the table, hoping his hungry gaze had cooled. He stepped back, trying for a haughty expression. "I am Officer Bischoff and I am your case officer in this case." He gave an inward wince at the repetition, the haughtiness slipping. He sounded stupid, tongue-tied.

But Ruben appeared oblivious to the embarrassing burble. He rocked back in his chair and tilted his head to one side, his brow furrowed as he appeared to look at something behind Victor.

Refusing to rise to the bait, Victor slipped off his jacket and hung it over the back of his chair. He straightened his shirtsleeves and strolled around the room, examining the heater and the thin grey woolen blanket on the bed before he crossed to the window to study the view.

Turning, he gazed at the sweep of Ruben's naked back. A thud of excitement made him shiver as he stared at the stumpy remains of a pair of angel wings. He remembered the wings on the plasticised exhibit he'd seen a decade ago—huge, outspread, the feathers the same colour as a barn owl's plumage, snowy white underneath and toffee speckled with dark splotches on top. From the tattered remains of Ruben's wings, they'd been white and blue-black. Just the idea of them took his breath away.

"Ruben Patrick Barbosa," he said, more to feel the shape of the name spoken aloud than for any other reason.

Ruben didn't turn around. He put both feet on the table. "That's me."

Victor went towards him, his gaze still fixed to the wing-stumps. "Why Patrick?"

A snort. "My father is pretentious."

"I thought perhaps he named you so because you were precious to him."

"I'm his firstborn. That's all." Ruben shrugged. The action made the stumps of his wings lift.

Unable to resist, Victor went closer. He reached out, wanting to touch the stubby feathered limbs, but snatched his hand away at the last moment. From this angle, he could see the bone within the layers of skin and feathers. For all his extensive reading on the architecture of angel wings, nothing had prepared him for this. Victor longed to trace the downy fluff around the base of the wings where they fused with the shoulder-blades, or to stroke the long muscles that ran either side of the spine.

He peered closer at where the wings had been amputated. A single stroke, cleanly done, shearing through the flesh and bone. There was no blood and no puckered flesh to suggest post-trauma cauterisation. Victor murmured, "This is why you fell."

Ruben rocked back on the chair so violently that Victor jumped aside. Turning, Ruben gave him a savage look. "You think?"

Victor blushed. "I'm sorry. Does it hurt? Have you had medical attention?"

"Buttercup, I haven't had any kind of attention since you people dragged me here. Of course it fucking hurts! How would you like it if your wings were suddenly chopped off mid-flight?"

"I don't have wings." Retreating from Ruben's anger, Victor perched on the edge of the table and arranged his pencils in neat alignment with his papers and reports.

"You don't?" Ruben stared, his gaze narrowing as if he could see through the sensible blue cotton of Victor's shirt. "I thought all demons had wings."

"Only those over second rank."

Ruben huffed and folded his arms across his chest as he resumed rocking on the chair. "Great. So I'm not even considered important enough to get a decent-ranking case officer."

Annoyed by his attitude, Victor slid off the table. Time for his training to come into play. Walking around the subject in a vague yet threatening manner often produced results—or at least it did when applied to exhausted, terrified humans desperate to claim asylum. Victor adopted his most officious tone. "I assure you, Mr. Barbosa, your case is being taken very seriously."

Ruben dropped his head backward to watch him stride to and fro. "Stop calling me that. Mr. Barbosa is my father."

"It would hardly be proper for me to call you by your personal name."

"Are you always this stuffy, buttercup?"

"Officer Bischoff," Victor corrected, and was rewarded with the flash of a smile that did strange things to his insides. He gritted his teeth against the lurch of physical reaction. He didn't want to be attracted to the subject. It was only natural he should be fascinated, of course, but anything else...

He came to stand directly behind Ruben. Avoiding the challenge in his dark gaze, Victor deliberately stared at the wing-stumps. As he moved closer still, he noticed the wave of goose bumps wash over Ruben's skin. Though half-naked, Ruben's body heat was more than noticeable, and so the goose bumps weren't caused by the cold.

Intrigued, Victor leaned down. His focus changed, snapping back to the wing-stumps as he neared them. His breath stirred the tiny rows of downy white feathers. The insane urge to kiss the stubs almost overcame him. He could picture himself doing it, running his tongue up the length of the stump and over the sheared top, tasting the sheen of the feathers. He wondered what it would be like to take the injured stumps one at a time into his mouth to suck on them. Would Ruben like it, or—

As if he could read Victor's mind, Ruben fidgeted in his seat. His nipples budded into hard peaks and a fresh scatter of goose bumps appeared on his tawny flesh. For a moment, Victor was confused, and then he realised it wasn't the cold making Ruben react, it was him. Delight at his power over the subject, however tenuous, made Victor lower his voice to a husky whisper. "Are you cold, Mr. Barbosa?"

Ruben sucked in his breath and jolted forward, banging his elbows against the table. He lifted his right shoulder as if he could rid himself of the ticklish murmur of Victor's voice and shivered, the stumps of his wings flexing involuntarily. "Are you one of those disgusting perverts who gets off on amputated angel wings, Officer Bischoff?"

"No." Victor straightened up. "I'm so sorry. That was crass and unforgivable."

The chair scraped back as Ruben balanced it on one leg. "Damn, you're cute. It's too easy to tease you." He laughed, but Victor saw a flicker of panic behind his eyes. Regardless of his bluster, the subject was afraid—and that knowledge made Victor's job easier.

"This dump is fucking freezing," Ruben continued as Victor moved around the table and pulled out his own chair. "It must be minus twenty outside and all I've got is a crappy two-bar heater!"

Victor straightened his papers once again and pursed his lips. "I will get you some more suitable clothing."

"You could be a gentleman and give me your jacket," Ruben said, pointing at the garment hanging over the back of Victor's chair.

Shooting him a suspicious look, Victor half rose and emptied his jacket pockets before handing it over. He should have thought of that before. It would be much easier to concentrate when Ruben was almost completely dressed.

Ruben stopped swinging on his chair and put on the jacket, murmuring at its cut and quality. "Warm," he said, pleasure in his voice as he snuggled into it. "Wool lined with layered satin. Nice." He tugged the jacket across his chest, his expression turning comical when the garment didn't meet across his torso. "Uh, you're slimmer than me."

Victor bit his lip to stop his laughter. "Sorry."

"At least it smells of you." Ruben burrowed his nose into the inside collar of the jacket and inhaled deeply. "Ah, God. You smell good, buttercup. Like— like pebbles in a sunlit stream. The first frost of autumn. Olive oil on old gold. The full heat of day on marble. Honeysuckle and sea grass."

Victor stared, the words echoing around his head. He'd never heard anything like it before, and while he knew it was probably just a devious angel trick, he was flattered and touched and wanted to hear more.

Blinking, Ruben lifted his head from the jacket, a blissful look on his face. "Oh, yes. You smell wonderful. I'd like to—" He stopped, as if suddenly remembering where he was, and he cleared his throat. "Never mind."

Even though he knew he was fishing for compliments, Victor couldn't help it. "You could really smell all that, just from the collar?"

"Yes. It was my—" Again Ruben stopped himself. His gaze went dead and he turned away. "Anyway, this should be enough to keep me warm until you get me some more clothes."

Victor had the feeling that Ruben was about to say 'my job'. He frowned as he opened the dossier and flicked through the pages. There was nothing there about Ruben having a job, unless being an obscenely wealthy playboy was considered a career.

Turning to a fresh page, Victor checked his watch

and made a note of the time. "Let us begin properly. Three days ago, you fell from the sky and struck the ground just south of the castle at Hämeenlinna. Eyewitnesses describe your arrival as a crash landing. You were out of control and travelling at a reckless speed that endangered humans and demons alike."

He paused and glanced up. "Of course, if your wings had been amputated, you would have had no control over your speed or flight path."

Ruben raised his eyebrows. "Of course."

The brittle response told Victor that their fleeting moment of bonding over the jacket had ended. With a sigh, he continued, "You caused approximately five thousand Euro in damage to real estate, which is usually chargeable to the perpetrator of said damage, except in those instances where it can be proven beyond reasonable doubt that the perpetrator was in fact a victim."

"I'm a fucking victim." Ruben leaned forward and flexed the stubs of his wings. "Look at me. Don't I look like a poster child for victimised angels?"

Victor ignored him. "Under Article 27a, sub-section B2 of the unilateral agreement between the DTM and the FIA, you have knowingly or unknowingly entered a restricted zone without due authority or cause and without the necessary documentation, governmental or magical, which therefore means we can detain you for an indefinite period while we conduct our investigations. Do you understand your rights?"

Ruben snorted. "Yeah. I'm stuck in this dump."

"We will—I will endeavour to make your stay as comfortable as possible." Victor initialed the page and tucked it beneath the dossier. Opening his notepad, he held the pencil ready. "Now, do you have anything you wish to say about the circumstances of your arrival in DTM territory?"

"I don't remember anything."

Victor referred to a page in his dossier. "The police report states you were unconscious when you landed."

"Yeah." Ruben swung back on his chair and folded his hands across his belly.

Victor stared at his interlaced fingers, the skin a slightly darker golden tan than the flesh of his torso. His gaze traced the arrow of dark hair from just below his throat down to his chest, then to where it narrowed into a downward stripe. He wondered if it felt as soft as it looked; how it would feel beneath his hand, beneath his lips...

With an inward curse, Victor snapped his concentration back to the interrogation. "Uh, when you say you don't remember, do you mean you don't remember the crash or you don't remember the events leading to the crash?"

Ruben brushed down the sides of the jacket, which fell open to reveal his chest. He gave Victor a gentle smile, as if well aware of the effect he was having. "Both."

"I see." Victor made a shorthand note then stared at it, wondering what the Hell he'd written. His pulse thumped and he shifted in his chair, uncomfortably aware of Ruben's body wrapped in his jacket. It seemed too intimate, and he wanted to demand his jacket back, but the idea of Ruben removing the garment made Victor's cock harden.

"So you're claiming you have amnesia?" His voice came out strangled. Victor swallowed thickly and pulled the notepad into his lap in a feeble attempt to hide from himself the evidence of his own arousal.

Ruben leaned forward, a lock of hair falling into his eyes. "Listen, buttercup—"

"Officer Bischoff." Victor pressed down hard with the pencil and swore as the tip broke off and skittered across the table.

"I prefer 'buttercup'." Again came that infuriating smile. "I can imagine you laid out in a meadow full of tall grass and wildflowers, your skin tanned pale gold and your hair kissed by the sunlight..."

The pencil snapped in two. Victor looked down at it and whimpered. He had to get a grip on himself. Oh God, that was entirely the wrong thing to think. He wriggled, his cock aching as it pressed against the restrictive seam of his trousers. Taking a deep breath, he discarded the broken pencil and picked up another. "As we were saying..."

"You. Naked. In a meadow." Ruben's expression turned dreamy for a moment before he sat up straight. "Do you even have meadows in this benighted country? All I could see was snow and lakes and snow and more snow."

Victor jumped on the admission. "So you do remember your fall!"

"Shit." Ruben chewed his lower lip, a frown wrinkling his brow. "Yes, I do. Everything until the actual impact, anyway."

Assuming a blank look, Victor doodled in the corner of his notepad. He had to play this cool. If Ruben could describe some of the landscapes he'd passed over on his ill-fated flight, a trajectory could be extrapolated to determine his point of origin. "What else did you see, apart from lakes and snow?"

"All sorts of things." Ruben shrugged and leaned back, tucking his hands behind his head. The jacket fell open again, exposing the full length of his torso.

Victor stared for a nanosecond then ducked his head, shading in his doodles with rapid strokes of the pencil. Another whimper threatened to break free of his throat. The sensible thing to do would be to lift his chin, breathe deeply, and get on with the next question as the training manual instructed, but he didn't think he could trust himself when such a luscious, tempting angel sat across from him.

Ruben tapped his fingers against his thighs. "I can see your horns, but where's your tail?"

"Excuse me?" Victor looked up, dropping the pencil to put a hand over one of his horns in a protective gesture. Demon horns were tiny things, perhaps two inches tall and with rounded ends. Many demons, especially those who worked in close proximity to humans, wore their hair styled to cover their horns. Some demons even had their horns surgically removed, as scientists had declared them to be as useless as the appendix.

"Your horns are kind of sweet." Ruben grinned. "I almost didn't see them in all that golden hair. So where's your tail?"

Victor felt himself blush. A demon's tail was an intimate appendage, and only an untutored innocent—or an ignorant fool—would ask such a personal question.

Apparently unperturbed by the silence, Ruben sat sideways on his chair and peered under the table. "You do have a tail, yes? All demons have tails."

"My tail is none of your business." Retrieving the pencil, Victor glared at him. "Answer the question, Mr. Barbosa. What did you see on your flight here?"

"C'mon." Ruben gave him a wicked smile. "I'll tell

you if you show me your little devil tail. Or do you have a big tail?"

Victor ground his teeth. The interrogation was spinning out of his control. He wouldn't get results this way, and he'd be disgraced in front of his peers and betters. Shame bit at him, and he let his temper slip, fixing Ruben with a warning look. "Stop this infantile behaviour, Mr. Barbosa. Answer the question. What did you see?"

Ruben's grin widened and he rocked forward, his eyes dancing with mischief. "First I want to see your tail. It's only fair. You've seen mine, now show me yours."

"No!" Victor banged his fists down on the table and swung to his feet, his chair knocked back with such force it overturned and crashed onto the floor. Rage and humiliation shook him. Victor stabbed a finger at Ruben, who shrank back, his bravado gone and a look of fear on his face.

"Do not ask about my tail, do you understand?" Victor barked. "Answer the fucking question! What did you see?"

A long silence followed. Ruben sat hunched in his chair, shivering uncontrollably, his eyes wide and his lips forming soundless words.

Victor stared at him. Had he really been that terrifying? Guilt replaced his anger, and he leaned across the table to apologise.

Ruben flinched from him.

Stunned by this development, Victor lifted his overturned chair and righted it. Just as he was wondering how to proceed, a pre-emptory knock sounded, and the door swung open. Emil Olsen stood on the threshold, his expression blank. "Officer Bischoff, a moment please."

Victor hesitated, his gaze going to Ruben, who remained frozen in his seat. "What about..."

"He'll be fine." Emil dismissed Ruben's obvious distress with a flick of the fingers. "Come with me, please, Officer Bischoff."

With a final concerned glance at Ruben, Victor followed Emil out of the room and down the corridor. Halfway along, Emil punched a code into a keypad and opened the door to the adjoining room. Inside it seemed to be a central research area, with a bank of telexes, computers, and telecast monitors. Two low-ranking demons paused in their tasks and stared at them with open curiosity.

Emil gestured at them. "Out."

The demons scuttled into the kitchen cubicle at the far end of the room, and soon came the hiss and gurgle of a coffee machine. Victor inhaled the rich aroma of the coffee and tried to ignore the demons watching through the kitchen window.

"Is that how they interrogate a subject in Britain?" Emil crossed the room to his desk and leaned against it. "I was told you were one of the best. Losing your temper with the subject is an amateur's mistake."

Victor drew himself up to his full height. Though he'd been seconded here, he was the same rank as Olsen and would not be spoken to like an inferior. "I apologise for the error. The subject asked about my tail."

Emil laughed. "So what? Show him your damn tail if he asks! We want him on our side. Do whatever it takes."

Not liking the tone of this conversation, Victor said coldly, "I'm not sure I understand what you mean."

"Do I have to draw a diagram?"

Emil sounded contemptuous. Feeling his anger rise again, Victor stalked over to the desk and faced him down, his gaze unwavering. "Maybe you should. I'm not resuming the interrogation until you tell me exactly what's going on."

An indefinable emotion glimmered in Emil's eyes. "Adolfo said you'd be like this. He said your father was a troublemaker, too. That's why they shipped him off to Monaco. All that sun... it must be a vile place. No one wants to go there, you know."

Victor ignored the jibe. He'd heard it all before,

the ignorance of northern demons for the southern countries of the DTM. Any land that shared a border with the FIA was seen as contaminated, and Monaco had long been disputed territory between angels and demons. Under DTM control now, it had been ruled by the angels only five years ago until a treaty brokered by Victor's father had returned the principality to the demons. The terms of the treaty favoured the DTM, so no one could understand why the FIA had agreed to sign it. As a result, conspiracy theories surrounded Valdemar and the treaty was the subject of much gossip and speculation.

Victor folded his arms, pleased when Emil backed off. "Draw me a diagram."

Emil muttered but retreated further, going over to a battered grey filing cabinet. He thumped the side and the middle drawer rolled forward, revealing an array of coloured files. Emil spent a moment searching through the folders before he removed a sheaf of photographs. He held them out. "Go ahead and look."

Taking them, Victor spread the pictures over Emil's desk. Though the images were grainy and obviously shot with a long-range lens, the detail was clear enough. "Where were these taken?"

"Ask your father."

"He took them?" Victor glanced up, but Emil's expression gave nothing away. Hiding his shock, Victor returned his attention to the photographs, which showed Ruben aboard a luxury yacht, presumably in the Mediterranean, alongside a succession of pretty blond boys. Ignoring the utterly ludicrous punch of jealousy, Victor studied Ruben's lithe, sexy body in the skimpiest of swimwear. He still had his wings in the pictures, the plumage banded white and blue-black like a magpie, and now Victor could see their full beauty as they furled and unfurled through the series of images.

He remembered that angels used their wings in sexual display as an indicator of arousal. His belly fluttered at the blatant telegraphing of desire echoed in Ruben's posture as he leaned towards a gorgeous blond human. Victor covered the image with another picture, this time showing Ruben in a passionate embrace with a blond angel whose kestrel-patterned wings splayed wide in invitation.

Victor picked up the photographs, flicking through them in silence. Most of the boys with Ruben were human, and as every demon knew, humans adored angels. Feeling slightly sick and depressed, Victor tossed the pictures aside and covered his face with his hands. He wondered how long ago those photographs had been taken, and if his father would tell him about it if he asked.

Valdemar had known he was being seconded to Station H. Victor had called him just after receiving his summons. Did his father know that he was coming here to interrogate Ruben? It seemed too much of a coincidence to keep it in the family like this. Valdemar had photographed Ruben for a reason, and now Ruben was under Victor's care... Something felt wrong about this, no matter which way Victor looked at it.

"Now do you understand?" Emil gathered the pictures together and returned them to the filing cabinet.

"Only that my father is involved in this." Victor wondered how best to phrase the next question. "Is he under investigation?"

Emil sighed. "Surely you can't be as dumb as you look."

Victor blinked. "Excuse me?"

"I show you photos of our fallen angel frolicking with pretty blond boys, and you're still asking me why you're the case officer? Un-fucking-believable."

Realisation hit him so hard, Victor felt winded. "You want me to be a honey trap."

"Hardly a trap. He's already stuck here," Emil said, rolling his eyes. "We just need you to be his honey."

"But... I didn't come here for that." Flustered, Victor followed Emil from the filing cabinet to the desk. "I don't have that kind of training."

Emil gave him a magnanimous smile. "Relax. It won't be difficult. He's young, good-looking, and vulnerable—how much of a hardship can it be to bed him?"

Victor felt himself blushing helplessly again. Of course he was attracted to Ruben. Of course he'd imagined what it would be like to have sex with him. Of course he'd memorised every inch of that perfect tawny body so he could jerk off thinking about him later on tonight—but that didn't mean he'd actually take the opportunity to sleep with him. The thought of being naked alongside Ruben, the thought of feeling his body pressed tight against him, made Victor's nerves shrivel even as it turned him on.

"I can't," he said, hearing the raw note of longing in his voice. He coughed to hide it. "Why don't you do it?"

Emil sat behind his desk, spread his hands, and assumed a regretful expression that wouldn't have fooled a five-year-old. "He doesn't fancy me."

"He might not like me, either!"

"Don't be stupid. Do you really think the Controllers would order you over here on the off-chance that Barbosa Minor might desire you?"

The word gnawed at him. Desire. Victor swallowed, heat sparking through him at the thought of the angel wanting him. He struggled to focus. "I can believe anything of the Department. They've done crazier things in the past."

"They knew what they were doing this time." Emil

pointed a finger at him and winked. "Not only do you fit the profile of Barbosa Minor's past lovers, we know he has a very strong physical reaction to you."

Victor felt his stomach drop out. Dizziness swam through his vision and he blinked, determined to hold on to the remaining shreds of his sanity. "He—he does?"

Emil thumped his desk and a video screen popped up. Pulling a wonky-legged keyboard towards him, he hit a few buttons and a live feed of Ruben's room emerged from the snow of interference.

"You're taping the interrogation." Victor couldn't keep the hurt and accusation from his voice.

Emil dropped his sharp-edged humour for a moment. "It's too damn important to leave anything to chance," he said softly. "Do you understand?"

Victor nodded.

Businesslike once more, Emil keyed in another command. "We monitored his heart rate and core body temperature. Angels have faster pulses and higher body temperatures than demons, but even so, there was a definite spike when you first entered the room. See here." He indicated the graph, where two wiggly lines coloured red and yellow meandered across the screen until they made a sudden jagged upward swing that almost went off the scale.

"And here again," Emil continued, his voice

cheerful as he scrolled through to the next graph. "This was when he asked about your tail."

Victor pressed his fingers to his cheek, trying to hold back the blush of shame and arousal. He cleared his throat as he straightened. "Will you record everything?"

"Yes."

"Everything?" Victor asked again, as delicately as possible.

"If necessary." Emil's eyes were cold.

Victor exhaled. "I'd like it to go on the record that I'm uncomfortable with this. I don't want to be recorded in—in compromising situations with the subject."

Emil snorted. "Listen to you! Anyone would think you were a shy little virgin."

Victor placed his hands on the desk and leaned forward. "I do not want to be taped having sex with the subject."

A smirk played at the edges of Emil's mouth. "You'll do as the Department orders, Officer Bischoff. If they want you to fuck him, you'll fuck him—and you'll like it."

CHAPTER 3

Ruben waited for five minutes before he moved. He didn't trust these demons not to be taping him or listening in on him somehow, even though he'd checked for A/V spy bugs as soon as he'd been shown into this room by drably-dressed demons and told it was his new temporary home. They hadn't told him why it was temporary, but Ruben assumed it was either because they were planning to move him into better quarters after the preliminary interrogation, or because they were planning on killing him.

He hoped it was the former.

Keeping a wary eye on the door, he pushed back his chair and stood. Officer Bischoff's jacket settled around him, warm and soft-scented. Ruben smoothed down the wool over his chest, enjoying the sensation of the satin lining over his bare skin.

His moment of pleasure was brief. With a frown,

Ruben wandered over to the window and stared out at the unprepossessing view. A high-walled garden with about a dozen spindly, dormant fruit trees met his gaze. Snow blanketed the ground, hiding who-knew-how many devices designed to keep intruders out and prisoners in. Beyond lay a black and tangled scrap of woodland. Above it all, the slate-grey sky glowered, the feeble sun trapped in a swaddling layer of cloud.

Horrible place. Horrible country. Even though he was warm, Ruben shivered. The action made the stumps of his wings rub against the jacket, reminding him of his failure.

He had no clear idea of what had happened to him, but he knew slightly more than he was prepared to tell the demons. Ruben replayed the events of the last few days, trying to make sense of them.

He'd been asked to accompany Valentin Tristan, a human coffee scientist, from Rio de Janeiro to Barcelona. Valentin had leave owing to him, and he'd filled out a government request for a one-month exit pass from South America so he could visit his family in Spain.

Though Valentin worked for Ruben's father, he lived at the mansion of the Rio Resident, Marc Soto. Popular opinion held that Marc wanted Valentin around for more than the perfect blend of morning coffee, but Ruben paid very little attention to gossip. As someone who hit the headlines on a weekly basis, he'd ceased to have any interest in rumour and couldn't care less who was doing what with whom.

He liked Marc, who'd never treated him with disdain because of his father, and who'd never tried to suck up to him for the same reason. Sometimes Ruben thought Marc was the only decent angel left in the South American FIA government, so when he'd received a telex from Marc asking if he'd make sure Valentin arrived in Spain safely, Ruben agreed.

After all, it wasn't that unusual a request—many angels who'd formed special connections with humans had the habit of trying to keep their humans safe and well, especially when aeroplane travel was involved. Since the war, the manufacture of planes, rockets, and other airborne devices had been banned by joint FIA-DTM agreement. As a result, air travel was an increasingly risky mode of transportation as the fleets got older and replacement parts became obsolete.

Like most angels, Ruben disliked sitting in the cramped quarters of an aeroplane. He hated the tiny seats and the way he had to crush up his wings, and the fact that he couldn't see where he was going always made him jittery. So as soon as Valentin boarded his flight, Ruben spread his wings and took off, heading up through the atmosphere to wait for the aeroplane to level out at its cruising altitude.

Now his breath clouded against the window, fogging his view of the winter garden. Ruben put out his hand to wipe away the mist, then jerked back. The glass was cold to the touch, and the residual heat of his skin left a fading smudge on the window. He gazed at the garden, noticing a set of neat tracks through the snow. An animal, no doubt—perhaps a fox. He had no idea what kind of creatures lived here.

He let his thoughts resurface, calling back the memory of his flight to Spain. It had been uneventful and dull until they'd headed into a storm somewhere over the Atlantic. He remembered it black with churning clouds, electricity crackling the air and the sky lit with violent flashes of lightning. The clouds swirled wetly about the plane, and a spiraling wind buffeted Ruben as he flew, tossing him first one way and then the other.

At first it had been fun, but as the storm worsened and his wings became drenched and his clothes stuck uncomfortably to his skin, Ruben grew tired. Mindful of his duty, he'd kept a dogged watch on the plane. The clouds blinded him, streaming water blurring his vision, and then the plane suddenly banked and dropped away as if trying to escape the storm.

He'd dived after it, his heartbeat drumming in his ears and his breathing harsh and rapid as he'd folded back his wings to ensure maximum speed.

A second later, agony screamed through him—a vivid, shocking pain of white heat. It lasted only a moment, like a single stroke of a razorblade through naked flesh, and then a horrific grinding ache filled every fibre of his being.

Ruben shuddered at the recollection. Even now he

felt the echo of his panic, the jagged spikes of his howling terror. He could still feel the heat of his blood spattered across his back and the jet of fluid found only within angelic wing structure. He tumbled head over heels, faster and faster, but didn't truly understand what had been done to him until he tried to spread his wings and slow his descent.

Only then, when they sheared away from his body in a mess of blood, bone, and wet feathers, did he realise that his wings had been cut off.

Ruben balled his hands into fists, his gorge rising. That moment of sheer, heart-stopping terror would stay with him forever. The knowledge that he was thirty thousand feet in the air and dropping like a stone, with no way of saving himself. He would never forget it, and would never forgive whoever had taken his wings from him.

He'd seen the sleek white shape of the plane tilt past him, but he didn't care. It barely even registered. The only thing he focused on was the wild beating of his heart and the hollow anguish inside him as he prepared to meet the reality of his death.

Pushing himself away from the window, Ruben took a deep breath and forced himself to relax. The demons would love it if he fell apart now. Their job would be so much easier if he broke down and told them everything. As it was, he had very little to tell them that they'd find useful, but they didn't need to know that just yet. He had to be strong and smart, and keep the demons at arm's length until he knew how to bargain his way back home.

Besides, someone was looking out for him. Ruben knew this with utmost certainty. How else had he got from midway over the Atlantic to the frozen wastes of Finland, if someone hadn't been controlling the whole thing? There were certain spells all angels were taught from childhood, spells of transportation that enabled them to relocate from one place to another, but Ruben hadn't been able to remember a single word of the spells during his fall. He'd simply been too scared.

And yet here he was, without his wings and a prisoner of the DTM, but alive and well. He'd been shorn of any ability to spell-cast himself out of there—the loss of his wings weakened the faint glimmer of magic he possessed—but he was still fit and healthy. Someone had spell-cast him out of that storm and hurled him into a low, swift descent into Finnish territory. It couldn't be down to pure chance that he'd been saved. There must be some meaning behind it, some reason he'd been sent here—though what that reason might be, he had no idea.

He only wished he'd been told about this beforehand. Did Marc know? Did Valentin? And what had happened to the aeroplane?

Ruben wriggled his bare toes on the paint-spattered floorboards and dug his hands in Officer Bischoff's jacket pockets. His fingers brushed against paper. Curious, he drew out his hand and looked at the scrumple of a spell-cast permission slip. Ruben pursed his lips as he smoothed out the paper and studied the lines of script written upon it: Radcliffe Camera to Helsinki Railway Station. Valid in one direction only for a period of three days from the date stamped below. Unauthorised travelers will be answerable to the Ministry of Justice.

A slow smile spread across his face. So, Officer Bischoff had been sent here from Radcliffe Camera, wherever that was, to interrogate him. Ruben felt slightly more cheerful, even though he supposed he should be even more wary.

He returned the permission slip to the pocket and strode over to the two-bar heater. For a moment he warmed himself, then he returned to his chair. Officer Bischoff had left his notes and dossier when he'd gone out of the room. Ruben doubted he'd find anything of interest inside, but took a quick look anyway. He snorted at the line of doodles on the notebook with the heavy shading and the preponderance of phallic-looking pyramids and cylinders. Oh, yeah. Officer Bischoff was hot. Correction: Officer Bischoff was hot for him.

Ruben's wing stumps wriggled with glee. There were three things he knew he was good at: his nose for blending coffee, his ability to piss off his father, and sex. He was very good at sex. His appetite for pretty blond boys irritated the Hell out of his father, which was a bonus, but mainly he liked to fuck because then he didn't have to talk.

Ruben wasn't very good at talking. Even dirty talk

was a problem. Not that any of his lovers seemed to care, because they always responded with such enthusiasm. Sometimes he wondered what was the biggest turn-on for them—the fact that he was the heir to one of the wealthiest angels in the FIA, or the fact that he was so silent in bed. He imagined it was the money.

Pretty blonds liked it when he flashed his cash. Doubtless Officer Bischoff would like it, too. Damn, but he was gorgeous, even if he was insanely repressed and corporate, the perfect image of a good, hard-working little demon.

Ruben had made it his own personal mission to seduce good boys, and with a happy sigh he started to weave a steamy fantasy involving himself and Officer Bischoff aboard his yacht as they cruised to the most exclusive Mediterranean party spots. Oh, how he'd love to get Officer Bischoff out of his boring demon clothes and into something sexier. Maybe then he'd get to see Officer Bischoff's tail. Ruben purred at the thought. He'd never had a demon in his bed before, and he was eager for the experience.

Just as his fantasy was heating up nicely, the door clicked open and Officer Bischoff entered. He locked gazes with Ruben for a heartbeat then looked away, a blush warming his face. He carried a pile of clothes in his arms, which he dumped onto the narrow bed. "At least some of these things should fit you."

Ruben got up and went over to the bed, deliberately standing too close. Officer Bischoff inhaled sharply but didn't move away. Ruben interpreted this as a good sign. He'd never had trouble attracting playmates before, and he was determined that no mere demon would resist him. Officer Bischoff's sexy body would be his for the taking by the end of the week. Ruben almost bounced on his toes at the thought.

When Officer Bischoff gave him a weird look, Ruben restrained his desire and poked through the garments without enthusiasm. At length he held up a shiny orange t-shirt and assumed a suitably disgusted expression. "This is nylon."

Officer Bischoff blinked. "So?"

"So I can't wear nylon. It's cheap and nasty." Ruben showed his disdain by throwing the t-shirt onto the floor and treading on it.

Officer Bischoff stifled a sigh. "I doubt we have silk and satin on hand."

"You could buy me some clothes," Ruben suggested wickedly, enjoying the sudden flush of colour on Officer Bischoff's pale cheeks. "Wouldn't you like that? This freezing country must have clothes shops, even if it only sells wolf-skin jackets and reindeer-pelt trousers. Go shopping and buy me something warm, buttercup, something soft I can wear next to my bare skin, something..."

"Not 'buttercup'. Address me as 'Officer Bischoff'." His face was flaming now, and he turned his head, his hair falling forward to conceal his expression. "I don't have the authority to buy you new clothes, although there's a limited budget allowance—I can make enquiries..."

"You enquire. I'm okay with linen, too. Egyptian cotton at a push." Ruben grinned when Officer Bischoff peeked back at him, his expression aghast. "I'll even let you take my measurements."

With a sniff, Officer Bischoff tossed his head, pushing back the wings of his sun-streaked hair with one hand. Ruben wondered where he could possibly have seen the sun. Certainly not in this benighted country; maybe wherever Radcliffe Camera was located had better weather.

Before Ruben could continue this line of thought, Officer Bischoff selected a pink shirt and thrust it at him. "I'll see about buying you some clothes, but for now, put something on before you catch a cold."

Ruben studied the pink shirt, which looked three sizes too big, before replacing it on the bed. "It's not that bad. I can sit here like this." He tugged at the collar of the jacket, flashing a goodly portion of his naked chest.

Officer Bischoff made a sound like a blocked drain.

"Why are you in such a bad mood, buttercup—I mean, Officer Bischoff?" Ruben gave him a huge, disingenuous smile. "Surely it's not because of me."

"Actually..." Officer Bischoff wavered, then glanced away, his mouth twisting. "I'm not happy about a certain aspect of my orders regarding you."

"They told you to show me your tail."

Colouring again, Officer Bischoff jerked his head up and glared at him. "And I told you, it's none of your business."

Ruben strolled over to his chair and leaned against its back. Folding his arms, he licked his lips and began a leisurely study of Officer Bischoff's body, putting as much blatant hunger into his gaze as possible.

Officer Bischoff's eyes flashed silvery fire. "Stop looking at me like that."

"I like what I see." Ruben smiled slowly. "The only demons I've met before were old and ugly, friends of my father. You're blond, slender, packed, and pretty. Just my type. That's why they brought you here, wasn't it?"

The look Officer Bischoff sent him could have frozen lava. "I have no idea what you're talking about. But now you've mentioned your father and his demon friends, let's discuss them..."

Ruben narrowed his gaze. "Let's not."

But Officer Bischoff looked thrilled, his eyes sparkling and a spring in his step as he strode around to the other side of the table and grabbed his notebook and a new pencil. "According to your dossier, your father is Ruben Barbosa Senior, Controller South for the FIA and a first rank angel. His wealth and power are inestimable..."

Ruben turned to face him, rolling his eyes and fake-yawning.

Officer Bischoff sent him an irritated look but continued, "It's also known that your father is in continual disagreement with the Deputy Director-General of the FIA, Joseph Cabrera, and that the Director-General Anton Rasmussen allows their battles to be waged openly."

"If you know all this, why do you need me?"

Officer Bischoff gave him a blinding, beautiful smile. "Ah, but how much do you know, Ruben?"

Reeling from the impact of that smile and the sound of his name on those pretty lips, Ruben sank down into his seat and gurgled. Damn, he was hard already and just from a smile. He had no doubt that Officer Bischoff was a real firecracker in bed. Ruben took a deep breath to calm his rioting thoughts, forcing his mind away from the question. His libido clamoured at him to answer truthfully, for surely if he did so, he'd be rewarded with Officer Bischoff's warm, willing body in his bed that very night.

But then Ruben reminded himself that he'd been sent here for a reason, and blabbing about his father's business deals and passing on trade information was probably a bad idea. With an effort, he silenced his lust and changed the subject completely. "You don't speak Finnish."

Apparently startled by the non sequitur, Officer Bischoff snapped, "I ask the questions."

"That was a statement."

With an aggrieved sigh, Officer Bischoff put down his notepad and pencil and massaged his temples.

"Before we continue with all the heavy stuff, I just want to know about your tail." Ruben adopted an innocent look, hiding his amusement at the blush creeping once more across Officer Bischoff's face. "I thought demons cut holes in their trousers so their tails could wave around."

Officer Bischoff's tight jaw made his words come out clipped. "Maybe in the olden days, but that hasn't been the custom for a long time. A demon's tail is his private business. We keep them wrapped around our legs. All right? Now you know."

Intrigued, Ruben put his head to one side and stared across the table at him, assessing the cut of his trousers. "Which side do you dress, buttercup?"

"You're impossible. This is impossible." Officer Bischoff slammed his hands down on his papers, then collected them together, his movements sharp and rigid.

Ruben laughed. He waited until Officer Bischoff had marched stiffly to the door before he called him back. "By the way, when are you going to fuck me?"

Officer Bischoff stared, his face ashen. "What?"

His smile gentle, Ruben said, "They'll tell you to do it."

"They already did." Officer Bischoff's blush was fiery, his confusion adorable.

"And?"

His chin lifted. "I won't."

"Why not?" Ruben widened his eyes. "Don't you like me?"

Officer Bischoff's fingers tightened on the door handle, then he swung it open and left without another word.

"You forgot your jacket!" Ruben shouted after him before the door slammed shut.

In the silence that followed, he imagined Officer Bischoff dawdling out in the corridor, too mortified to come back in. Ruben chuckled. Oh, Officer Bischoff would be back, all right. He wouldn't be able to stay away.

Ruben snuggled into the jacket and gave a happy

sigh. He couldn't wait for the next day of interrogation.

CHAPTER 4

Victor cut the idling engine and the sound died away into silence. He sat for a moment, listening to the quiet grow heavy around him. His breath misted in the interior of the car as the residual warmth given out by the heater faded. Through the windscreen he saw the long, forbidding shape of the old prison with the rounded, red brick form of Hamë Castle behind it. Both were enclosed by a high wall and surrounded by a gentle, snow-covered slope. To his right, the frozen surface of Lake Vanaja glimmered in the sunlight.

The city of Hamënlinna lined one side of the lake at a visible distance from the castle. Victor lingered in the borrowed car for another few minutes, studying the landscape and the swathe of dark trees on the opposite side of Vanaja, then he opened the door and got out.

He sucked in a breath at the bite in the air and

cuddled deeper into his synthetic fur-lined coat. He'd left his nice warm jacket with Ruben, which had been a stupid mistake, but one he couldn't face rectifying just yet. The idea of going back into the interrogation room and dealing with that slow smile and those knowing, seductive looks, not to mention having to steel himself against the effect of that sexy body so willfully displayed...

Victor coughed, forcing his attention back to his surroundings. He really had to get this ridiculous case of lust under control. He'd always prided himself on his professionalism, and was determined that Ruben Patrick Barbosa wouldn't distract him from his job.

At least, that had been his mantra when he'd looked in the mirror this morning. Whether the mantra would work was another matter entirely.

Once he'd locked the car, Victor shoved his hands in his pockets and walked around the castle, his feet squeak-sliding through the fresh fall of snow. It had only been a couple of inches, so he was hopeful that the site of Ruben's crash landing would still be mostly undisturbed.

Rounding the wall towards the lakeside, Victor saw the fluttering strip of yellow and black tape cordoning off the area. A blue-uniformed policeman wearing a furry grey hat sat on a dusted-off picnic bench, the polystyrene cup of coffee in front of him melting a small circle in the snow on the tabletop. As Victor approached, the cop curved a hand around his coffee and stood to meet him, speaking in Finnish.

Victor flapped his hand in apology, dredging up the few limited phrases he remembered. "Anna anteeksi, en ymmärrä... Englantia?"

The cop seemed to understand. "English? Not a good time for tourist visit."

"I'm not a tourist." Victor pulled his ID from his inside coat pocket and held it up.

"Ah. Hold, please." The cop handed him the cup of coffee then took Victor's ID and examined it with interest, fingering the barcode and the glossy stamps of rank and clearance levels.

Victor breathed in the sweet scent of the coffee, his body reacting to the gentle suggestion of the drug. Though the cop's coffee was very milky and had far too much sugar in it for Victor's taste, just the smell set up a craving. He was glad to pass it back to the cop in exchange for his ID.

"A team from Helsinki were here until two days ago. Said they'd found everything." The cop looked at him with obvious curiosity. "It snowed last night."

Victor put on his most official smile and took a step towards the cordon. "I'm just following things up."

"Suit yourself." The cop shrugged. "Tell me if you find anything. I will have to call it in."

"No problem." Victor lifted the striped plastic tape and ducked beneath it, ignoring the weight of the cop's stare on his back. He couldn't blame the guy—it must be a boring duty—but he'd have preferred it if he didn't have an audience for his every move.

Victor wasn't even sure what he was looking for. It wasn't as if he could glean anything new from the site that hadn't already been described in mind-numbing detail in the police report. The sensible thing would have been to stay in the Turku safe house and continue the interrogation of the subject, but instead here he was at the scene of the crash, freezing his arse off in the snow.

He walked the area within the cordon, placing his footsteps with care. The impact crater was deeper than he'd imagined from reading the report, the hard earth churned up and turned over. Though wet with melting snow, the frozen mud still carried the imprint of Ruben's body.

Victor crouched beside the crater, his gaze riveted to the two sharp holes a hand's span apart. Ruben's wing stumps had made those holes, he realised, and a tremor went through him at the thought. He knew the DTM team had been over the ground already and taken swabs, but there was nothing in the dossier about blood or wing tissue. Ruben had told him the truth yesterday—his wings had been sheared straight off mid-flight. The fact that they'd healed without any kind of medical attention suggested that Ruben had been the victim of a magical attack—but who would do such a thing?

Blowing out a clouded breath, Victor got to his feet and resumed his walk. Demons and angels sometimes encountered one another in free air space, and occasionally they fought with one another. But to sever an angel's wings like that took skill. It didn't seem to be a random, opportunistic attack but rather something deliberate.

Ruben Patrick Barbosa had enemies, or so it seemed. Unless... Victor pondered, scrunching through older, ice-crusted snow as he approached a stand of trees. Unless Ruben wasn't the focus of the attack. Maybe whoever did this wanted to strike at Ruben's father, Barbosa Senior.

Victor stopped, staring unseeingly at the crystals of snow sprinkled on the evergreen pines in front of him. Could this have been a hit on behalf of the FIA's Deputy Director-General, Joseph Cabrera? Even though Ruben had intimated that he wasn't close to his father, he was still Barbosa Senior's heir. If Cabrera wanted to send a direct message to Barbosa Senior, surely he'd do it through an attack on Ruben.

Or was this all too obvious? Victor bowed his head, the wings of his hair falling forward to brush his cold cheeks as he paced back and forth, moving further beneath the trees. The snowfall was less thick here, and a mat of golden-brown pine needles broke the surface of white every now and then.

It would be easy enough for him to cross-reference FIA chatter from the time of the attack. If

Cabrera had planned the hit against Ruben, there'd be reference to it somewhere in all the information passed through the secure channels. Victor's job in Oxford was to record and sort through these data transmissions. Most were high-level encrypted, and it was his primary task to break the codes and retrieve the information so DTM operatives could act, especially if it involved the movement of refugees.

Victor paused beneath a tree and sighed, scraping his hair from his eyes. He needed to be back in Oxford to run those checks. There had to be something else he could do here and now to uncover the truth if he was going to be able to help Ruben.

Help him?

Blinking, Victor took a breath and leaned back against the tree trunk. He was supposed to be helping the Station H, not the subject. Shit! Where the Hell was his brain?

He exhaled, closing his eyes against a wash of embarrassment. He knew exactly where his brain was—in the gutter, where it was jelly-wrestling with his libido and having a fine old time.

Victor gritted his teeth as an onslaught of sexy images filled his mind. It was bad enough that he felt attracted to Ruben, but just to torture him even more, his unconscious had sent him a whole series of dirty, achingly hot dreams last night. He'd woken with his cock hard and his sheets damp with the spill of his seed. His cheeks burned at the memory. Wet dreams were for horny teenagers, not for sensible twenty-somethings intent on climbing the career ladder.

It was just a bad dose of lust. That was all. Victor scuffed through the pine needles beneath the tree and tried to convince himself again. It'd been a while since his last boyfriend. Actually, it had been more like eleven months and sixteen days since the last time he'd kissed a guy, let alone had any kind of sexual activity. He thumped his head back against the tree bark with a groan. No wonder he couldn't stop his rampaging hormones. He was ripe and prime for the plucking, and the fact that Ruben was an angel only made him all the more alluring.

It also made him terrifying. Victor opened his eyes and stared up through the spreading canopy of dark winter green. He felt intimidated by Ruben's status as much as by his experience. Those photographs Emil had shown him still haunted Victor. He blushed to recall how he'd fantasised about trading places with one of the pretty blond boys in the pictures, and how he'd imagined what it would be like to lie on the sun-drenched deck of the sleek yacht with Ruben's practically naked body pressed hotly against him.

Desire curled in his belly, and Victor jerked away from the tree, tamping down on his arousal. He resumed walking, suddenly aware of the policeman watching him from the picnic bench. Feeling self-conscious, he waved at the cop then turned his attention back to the snow-covered ground. Despite the fact that there was nothing to be found here, Victor didn't want to go back to Turku just yet.

He circled around the trees, kicking through a bank of snow. Spotting something, he knelt and dug until his fingers turned blue with cold, but only succeeded in excavating a soggy copy of a newspaper from six days ago. He dropped it back into the snow with a frustrated sound. This was useless. He was wasting time. Just because he didn't totally trust the motives of Station H didn't mean he should be out here shirking his duties.

Victor replayed the telephone conversation he'd had with his father this morning. He'd stopped in Forssa on his way from Turku to Hamënlinna and had called Valdemar from a public phone box outside a petrol station. When his father had chuckled at the basic security measure, Victor had said, "I'm worried, Dad. Worried they're trying to implicate you in something."

The chuckle became a laugh. "Let them try."

"But, Dad—"

"It'll be fine, Victor. Don't worry about it. Just do your job."

"What if I find something? Something incriminating."

After a long moment, Valdemar had sighed. "If you find something, you do your duty. Understand? Do your duty, and trust your instincts."

His father had hung up, leaving Victor feeling none the wiser.

He sighed and checked his watch, aware of the day fading into the afternoon twilight even though it was only just past noon. The brush of something cold and gentle against his face made him glance up, and he saw tiny snowflakes spiralling from a mass of grey clouds.

Time for him to head back to Turku. He had no desire to spend the rest of the afternoon stuck on the roads in a blizzard. As he cut through the stand of trees, Victor noticed the gleam of a feather trapped amongst some low-lying branches. He plucked it free as he passed and turned it in his hand, pausing beneath the canopy for a moment while he examined the feather.

Shiny and silvery white with a curl and splodge of inky blue-black, it was definitely not a bird's feather. Victor stared at it, wondering. He held it under his nose and above the musty smell of cold earth and damp trees, he caught Ruben's scent. Dark heat, bright sunshine and deep shadows, dusky seduction.

Victor turned his head sharply, his breath hitching in his throat. He didn't know how he'd picked up a scent from a lone feather that had been exposed to the elements for the past five days, but he knew beyond doubt that this particular feather had fallen from one of Ruben's wings.

He took an evidence bag from his coat pocket and

slipped the feather inside, then sealed it and tucked it into his inside pocket. Screw telling the cop about his find—it was just a feather. Victor wanted to keep it for himself.

The snow was falling thicker and faster as he left the cover of the trees. The cop had abandoned the picnic bench and stood sheltering against the castle wall. He lifted his hand as Victor bent beneath the cordon and trudged towards his car, and Victor gave him a quick salute in response.

As he neared his vehicle, Victor heard the muffled sound of the car phone. He fumbled the keys out of his trouser pocket and unlocked the door, sliding into the front seat and hitting 'answer'.

"Officer Bischoff, why are you in Hamënlinna?"

Victor sat up straight as he recognised the voice as belonging to Adolfo Oscar. "How do you know where I am?"

Adolfo made an amused sound. "Apart from the fact that all Station H cars are fitted with location-identifying transponders, the police officer on duty at Hamë Castle radioed in your interest in the site."

Annoyed, Victor glanced over at the cop huddled against the wall. "That was unnecessary."

"I decide what is unnecessary, Bischoff."

The hint of steel in Adolfo's voice made Victor

grimace. "Yes, sir."

"The police officer was only doing his job."

"So was I," Victor argued.

Adolfo snorted. "Indeed? Half a dozen field men searched the area exhaustively. There's nothing to find that hasn't been found already. Your job is to interrogate the fallen angel, not to play at being a field man. Your expertise is needed in other areas."

"So I've been told." Victor couldn't keep the sarcasm from his tone.

"You have a problem with your assignment, Bischoff?"

Victor bit his lip. He wanted to complain about the order to sleep with Ruben, but knew it would be hypocritical. "No, sir."

"Good. I'm glad you understand how important this is." Adolfo paused, and the line crackled faintly with a blur of static as the snowfall increased. "You didn't find anything out there, did you?"

Like Hell would he mention the feather now. "No."

Another crackle, then Adolfo said, "Get back to Turku and resume the interrogations. Controller Scandinavia wants an update and I've got nothing to tell him. I want results—and soon. I'll call again tomorrow."

Victor stifled a groan. "Yes, sir."

The line went dead, and the only sound was the soft thump of snow against the car roof. With a sigh, Victor started the engine and put the vehicle into reverse. It was going to be a long drive back to Turku.

CHAPTER 5

Ruben lay on the narrow bed and stared at the remnants of a dusty cobweb hanging from the ceiling. The spider had long since departed—probably it had died of boredom, stuck in this dump—but its web remained, strands of gossamer wafting in the cold draught that somehow crept through the closed window.

With a long-suffering sigh, he rolled over and kicked off the woollen blanket covering his body. He got out of bed and strolled naked across the room, running his hands through his hair and yawning. The pile of ugly clothes Officer Bischoff had given him two days ago tottered on the floor, and Ruben sorted through them with one foot before selecting a pair of grey cotton sweatpants.

He pulled them on, not bothering with underwear, then went over to the small washbasin and brushed his teeth just for something to do. His enforced stay in this shit-awful place was getting more tedious by the second, and he'd started contemplating doing something crazy, like smashing the window and jumping out, just to see what would happen.

Maybe boring him to death was part of the demons' cunning plan. Ruben rinsed out his mouth and replaced his toothbrush in the holder, then stared at his reflection in the fly-spotted mirror. He was wasting away in here. So many pretty boys to fuck, and he was here all alone, without even a porn mag to keep him company. Damn it, not even the sexy Officer Bischoff had come to see him yesterday.

Ruben dropped his gaze and looked at the small brown bottle full of sleeping pills prescribed by a human medic after Ruben had complained that the pain from his wing stumps hurt too much for him to sleep. He'd taken one last night, and the dull grinding ache had lessened enough for him to get some rest. Unfortunately, it didn't deaden his desire, and he'd enjoyed a long, slow, doped-up wank whilst thinking about Officer Bischoff naked and sweaty and writhing against leather restraints on silken sheets.

Hell, yeah. Ruben grinned at the thought, his body stirring in response. He smothered a laugh and pottered over to the window, looking out at the monotonous view. He missed his yacht and the taste of the sea breeze, the feel of the sun on his skin and the freedom of the ocean. This place looked like it saw the sun once a year, and he had no idea how far he was from the sea. In fact, he had only a sketchy idea of the geography of the Scandinavian DTM countries. He'd never had reason to pay the slightest bit of attention to anywhere so far north.

The door rattled, and he turned in time to see Officer Bischoff enter, laden down with bags imprinted with the word Stockmann.

Ruben beamed. "Hello, buttercup."

"Officer Bischoff," muttered Officer Bischoff, but he didn't sound so annoyed by the nickname this time.

"What's all this?" Ruben wandered over to take a look as Officer Bischoff pushed back the fake-fur collar of his ugly coat and upended a couple of the bags on the table.

"Clothes." Officer Bischoff cast him a disparaging glance, his gaze lingering over the planes of Ruben's naked chest. He licked his lips and blushed slightly before turning back to the bags. "I got permission to buy you some new things, so I went shopping. There's a winter sale on at Stockmann's."

"Great if you have a yen for grey," Ruben said, holding up a grey marl t-shirt in soft, warm cotton. Folded beneath it on the pile was a charcoal grey sweater with a single dove grey stripe and a pair of dark grey trousers.

Officer Bischoff looked up. "You don't like grey."

"I love it!" Ruben cuddled the t-shirt against his

cheek with the kind of delighted expression that wouldn't fool a three-year-old.

"There is also black." Officer Bischoff looked hurt, his eyes dulling slightly as he pushed another bag across the table.

"Grey and black. What the well-dressed Finnish demon is wearing this season." Ruben tried to keep his voice cheerful. Damn, he shouldn't have sounded so ungrateful. Now Officer Bischoff was mad at him.

"I bought you some books, too." Ignoring him, Officer Bischoff picked up one of the remaining bags and carried it over to the bed. He unbuttoned his coat before he started removing the books one by one and setting them on the wobbly bedside table. "I wasn't sure what you liked reading, so there's a selection of English-language stuff. I also found some in Portuguese. I hope that's all right."

"Portuguese?" Ruben stopped sorting through his new wardrobe. "You bought me Portuguese books?"

Officer Bischoff blushed again and nodded, allowing his hair to fall forward to obscure his expression. "You're Brazilian. I thought..."

"You thought right. Wow. You're really kind." Striding over, Ruben grabbed the book Officer Bischoff offered him. "I haven't read this one. Thanks."

"It's part of my job." Officer Bischoff sounded

stiff and formal.

Some of the joy ebbed out of Ruben. "Oh. Yeah. But thanks all the same." He started to move away, the book still clutched in his hand, when he smelled it—faint, almost untraceable, but he had a nose trained for the slightest nuance of scent, and he knew this smell intimately. The book dropped to the floor and he stared at Officer Bischoff, who had just finished building a tidy pile of the other books upon the bedside table.

Hearing the thud of the book on the floorboards, Officer Bischoff turned suddenly. His unbuttoned coat flared open with the movement and the scent struck Ruben again—unmistakable, a siren call of a fragrance.

"What..." Officer Bischoff began, but his question ended in an undignified squawk as Ruben tore off his coat, shoved him down onto the bed, and pounced on top of him.

The feel of Officer Bischoff squirming beneath him made Ruben hard in an instant. God, if only this was for fun—but there was something much more serious going on. Ruben tried to keep his mind focused even though his body clamoured lustfully for pleasure. Officer Bischoff struggled, outrage replacing shock, and he almost clouted Ruben around the head as he fought to escape.

"Buttercup, wait—it's not—" Ruben ducked as another punch grazed his jaw. Office Bischoff clearly wasn't going to listen to reason. Time for Ruben to take preventative measures. He shoved his weight through his hips, grinding his erection between Officer Bischoff's splayed thighs, then caught handfuls of Officer Bischoff's wash of golden hair to keep him still, and kissed him.

For a moment he felt only resistance, tasted only surprise. Officer Bischoff went completely rigid beneath him, his lips tight and tense and closed. Ruben felt the frantic thunder of his heartbeat and realised Officer Bischoff was holding his breath.

"Silly buttercup." Ruben lifted his mouth a fraction and heard Officer Bischoff gasp for air. Before he could recover enough to start squirming again, Ruben pressed a line of feather-light kisses over his lips, using every ounce of skill to make his reluctant captive relax. A moment later, he whispered very softly, "They're listening to us, aren't they?"

Officer Bischoff made a tiny sound that could have been affirmation.

"Kiss me." Ruben traced his lips over Officer Bischoff's mouth, waiting for a reaction. When none came, he continued in a normal tone of voice, "That bastard Olsen interrogated me yesterday. Where were you, Officer Buttercup?"

Officer Bischoff shifted beneath him. The confusion in his eyes faded to wariness and resignation, and he muttered, "Officer—oh, to Hell with it. My name is Victor."

"Mm, now we're getting somewhere. Victor." Ruben released the tight grip on Victor's hair and stroked back the golden strands, framing his face. He parted the hair around the tiny red horns and tested the rounded point of one with his thumb. "Funny how a demon has an angel's name. It's Greek, yes? 'Victory'. Your father must have had a sense of humour."

He leaned down and kissed Victor again, taking his time, enjoying the pretense of intimacy even if Victor kept his mouth firmly closed. Ruben wriggled, moving partway onto his side but keeping most of his weight sprawled lazily across Victor's body, effectively pinning him to the bed. He trailed kisses from Victor's mouth along his jaw then nuzzled through his hair to bite at his earlobe.

Victor made a choked noise and tried to break free, but Ruben clung tight. He knew he was taking a huge risk doing this. The listening devices might not be able to pick up his whispers, but there was nothing stopping Victor from reporting their conversation in its entirety. But Ruben needed to know, and Victor was the only one who could tell him, and so it was worth the risk.

Ruben licked the curve of Victor's ear and felt him tremble in response, heard his breath hitch. Choosing his moment, Ruben purred softly, soothingly, then whispered, "You have one of my feathers. I can smell it on you."

Victor gasped and jerked in reaction. He snapped his head towards Ruben and stared at him, his eyes wide with startled guilt and his lips forming a question. Before he could ask it, Ruben wedged himself onto his side and put his hand between Victor's thighs, his aim unerring. "Where is it?"

"Not down there!" Victor abandoned his own question as he tried to push Ruben away. He wriggled, his face red with embarrassment as each successive maneuver only seemed to bring him closer to Ruben's body.

Ruben ran his fingertips over the inside of Victor's legs, up then down, and drew in a breath when he felt the slight ridges of tail wrapped around his left thigh. It was almost as exciting as feeling the sudden thrust of Victor's erection tenting out the fabric of his trousers. Distracted, Ruben rubbed at the coiled length of tail then palmed Victor's cock, pressing down with the heel of his hand.

That got his attention. Victor moaned, his head going back and his eyes closing in brief surrender. Ruben kissed his throat as he worked his fingers over Victor's cock, teasing him through the layers of cloth separating their flesh.

"Please," Ruben murmured against his neck, "bring me the feather."

Victor gasped.

Ruben wasn't sure if that was in agreement or

refusal. He needed that feather for his wings to regenerate. It had to be a complete, full-fledged feather—the old wives' tales were specific on that count—and Ruben knew without doubt that Victor had one of his primary feathers in his possession. All he had to do was convince Victor to give him the feather, and then Ruben would be able to spell-cast a new pair of wings from it.

Not that he knew the correct spell for wing regeneration, but he'd deal with that particular hurdle when he came to it. First of all he needed to get the feather, then escape from this safe house, and then...

No. First of all, he needed to kiss Victor again.

Ruben crushed his mouth over Victor's, eating at him with hungry passion. Victor made a muffled moaning sound—the kind of sound Ruben was beginning to love more than anything else—and then he responded.

The kiss deepened. Victor opened his mouth and returned the embrace, no longer shy but aggressive and demanding. He bit at Ruben and thrust his tongue between his lips. Ruben chuckled, which seemed to make Victor lose even more control. Their breathing grew ragged as the kiss turned bruising and savage. Victor was angry, Ruben realised, and he started to pull back.

As soon as Ruben moved, Victor lifted both hands and braced them against Ruben's naked chest, trying to shove him away. But then his palms flattened and his fingers relaxed, and the tension in his arms loosened. The rejection became a welcome. Victor gave him a dazed, helpless look and stroked his hands over Ruben's chest, curling through the soft hair, caressing the sensitive peaks of his nipples.

Ruben groaned at the spark of pleasure. Wanting more, he grabbed Victor's hand and guided him down to his cock. Slow and tentative, Victor splayed his fingers and groped Ruben's erection through the thick cotton of the sweatpants. Victor's breath came in short, sharp bursts, his expression stunned, as if he couldn't believe what he was doing.

Ruben watched him, gasping as Victor's hand moved up and down his aching cock. When Victor's lips parted in unmistakable invitation, Ruben fell on him, his kiss ferocious and greedy, his tongue stabbing and plundering. Victor mewed and arched into it, his fingers squeezing Ruben's cock through the sweatpants.

"God, yes. Yes, buttercup."

Suddenly Victor jerked sideways, almost toppling from the bed. He wormed halfway from beneath Ruben and launched himself towards the floor, but Ruben seized him around the waist and hauled him back onto the mattress. Victor lashed out, panicking, and Ruben sat on him, catching both flailing hands and pressing them together, exerting just enough pressure on his wrists that Victor went still and stared at him.

Ruben wanted to reassure him, but the sight of Victor with his hair mussed and spread out against the blanket, his lips bruised from their kisses and a vulnerable look in his eyes made Ruben want to fuck him senseless. All this rough and tumble had made him as horny as Hell, and so Ruben forgot about reassurance and went for the direct approach. "Not so fast, sweetheart. You can't get me all hot and bothered and then just run away."

Victor continued to stare at him. Whereas a moment ago his expression had been one of fading fear, now his eyes glittered with defiant challenge. A flash of lustful delight shivered through Ruben as he realised Victor was enjoying this. Oh, he was still a repressed little good boy, but the wanton, wicked demon inside him was trying to break through.

Determined to win this particular battle, Ruben bent down and kissed him until Victor began to respond again. The fight went out of him and Victor made no resistance when Ruben unfastened his trousers and slid a hand inside. Victor canted his hips, rubbing against Ruben's exploring hand, then he went still as Ruben touched the muscled warmth of his tail.

It felt like nothing he'd imagined. Smooth and hard, like an erect prick, Victor's tail pulsed with heat and strength. Ruben stroked it, measuring its width— about the circumference of his thumb—by touch alone. He wondered how long it stretched, and was about to ask when he caught sight of the worry in Victor's expression.

Ruben swallowed. "Am I hurting you?"

Victor shook his head. "My tail doesn't disgust you?"

"You have got to be kidding." Ruben stared at him in genuine shock. "You have the sexiest tail I've ever seen. I mean, felt. Can I see it?"

"No!" Victor batted at his hands as Ruben tried to wrestle down his trousers. "Get away. Get off me. You can't..."

Amused by Victor's obvious conflict between desire and duty, Ruben gave a throaty laugh and moved his hand from tail to cock. Victor's erection was hard and fierce, the head leaking wetness over Ruben's fingers. Purring, he stroked its full length and watched Victor buck in reaction. "Oh, buttercup. Do you like this? Does it feel good?"

Ruben was surprised at the words tumbling from his lips. For someone usually so silent in bed, now he couldn't seem to shut himself up. Of course, it helped that Victor responded so beautifully. Ruben licked the line of his throat. "You taste so damn sweet. Never thought a demon would taste like Heaven."

Victor whimpered, his jaw tight and his head whipping from side to side while his hips thrust up, his cock hot and throbbing in Ruben's hand.

"What if I put my mouth on you?"

Victor's eyes opened wide. "No!"

Ruben inhaled deeply, enjoying the musky scent of their combined arousal, and sighed. "I wonder if your cock tastes as incredible as you smell. I can make it amazing for you. I'm really, really good at giving head."

"Oh, God—"

"Just one lick," Ruben coaxed, wriggling against him, rubbing his own erection against the taut muscle of Victor's thigh. "God, you're so hard. I can feel you leaking all over my hand. Let me have a taste."

Drawing his hand from inside Victor's trousers, Ruben lifted it to display the glistening wet trails of pre-cum. "Mm," Ruben murmured, and sucked his fingers. The smoky taste rolled over his tongue, making him crave more. "Oh, baby. I have got to have you. Got to make you come in my mouth. You taste so fucking good."

Victor stared at him, utterly speechless.

"C'mon. Let me do it." Ruben pulled back and tried once again to drag Victor's trousers down over his hips, but Victor made a desperate sound of protest and kicked out. Caught off-balance, Ruben fell sideways and banged his elbow against the wall. The sudden sharp pain distracted him for a second, and that was long enough for Victor to escape.

Holding up his trousers with both hands, Victor

backed across the room until he met the opposite wall. Only then did he put his clothes in order, his fingers shaking. "I'm sorry," he said, his voice full of unhappiness and panic. "I can't. I just can't."

"Why not?" Frustration scalded him. Ruben punched the thin mattress and growled as his fist connected with the hard wooden slats beneath. He flung himself from the bed and paced to the window, trying to regain some measure of control. "Damn it, Victor, why won't you let me fuck you?"

"I don't like playing games." Slumped against the wall, Victor trembled as if he was cold. "I—I'm a serious kind of guy. I only sleep with people I c-care about."

Ruben snapped around to stare at him. Realisation was slow, but the more he thought about it, the more obvious it became. Unable to keep the glee from his voice, he crowed, "Why, Officer Bischoff—you're a virgin!"

The look Victor shot him was full of fury and humiliation. "You're wrong."

In response, Ruben gave him a patient, gentle smile. "Oh, buttercup. You can't lie to an angel."

Horror registered on Victor's face for a split-second, but then he bared his teeth in a snarl. "Demons can lie to anyone. Even angels."

"So are you lying to me now?" Ruben paced

towards him, amused by Victor's confusion. "Prove me wrong. Sleep with me. Come on." Tilting his head, he ran his hands down his body and hooked his thumbs into the waistband of the sweatpants, pulling them low on his hips. "You want me. I know you do."

"I don't," said Victor, but his gaze was fixed to the waistband and the dark gloss of pubic hair revealed above the sweatpants.

Ruben smirked. "Look into my eyes and tell me you didn't dream about me last night."

Drawing in a deep breath, Victor lifted his head and stared at him. "What if I did?"

Ruben sighed and reached out for him as he went closer. "By every angel in Heaven, why are you being so stubborn? I can be everything you dreamed of— everything and more. I'll bring you such pleasure, Victor. I'll make it so good for you..."

Victor sidled away along the wall, a hunted expression on his face.

Ruben tried to corner him against the washbasin. "You're gorgeous, so fucking gorgeous," he whispered in honest admiration. "I want you so much. Come here—let me touch you—let me give you what you want..."

A hesitation, and then Victor threw him a stormy look. "Go to Hell," he snapped, and shoved past him.

He stamped across the floor, stopping only to grab his coat, and then rushed from the room. The door slammed shut so hard that the dusty cobweb dropped from the ceiling.

"Victor! You'll dream of me again and again until you give in!" Ruben shouted after him. "And you will give in, Officer Bischoff! I will have you!"

Whirling around, Ruben banged both hands against the wall then slid down onto his knees. He ached all over with frustrated desire, but worse, he'd scared off the closest thing he had to an ally in this horrible place. He curled up, shivering with reaction, as loneliness and fear overcame him.

CHAPTER 6

By the end of the week, neither the weather nor Ruben's mood had improved. The only bright spot in each day was his interrogation. He looked forward to it with a sense of excitement that far outweighed what he probably should be feeling for such an event. The FIA interrogations he'd been obliged to witness in the past because they were led by his father were always terrifying, tense, and very often violent—a far cry from this softly, softly approach the DTM were taking.

Of course, Officer Bischoff was the main reason Ruben got out of bed with a spring in his step, a smile on his face, and a scatter of crusted tissues tumbling to the floor. Victor continued to resist every attempt at seduction, no matter how blatant or subtle, and Ruben had resorted to questioning every other demon and human he saw as to what he was doing wrong.

No one had any useful suggestions for him, and

Ruben was feeling increasingly despondent. He knew Victor wanted him. The silly little demon was just being ridiculously stubborn. In return, Ruben dug in his heels and refused to give out any information about the FIA. He couldn't even be bothered to give them the disinformation all high-ranking angels were meant to spout at the enemy if they were ever captured.

Instead, he sniped at Victor, teased him, joked with him, and begged him to come to bed. Victor smiled patiently and looked at his watch and left the room whenever the conversation became too loaded with innuendo.

Ruben had had enough. He'd read two books and spent the evenings listening to Finnish radio after Victor had brought him a small wireless. Ruben had attempted to pick up longer-range broadcasts from outside the DTM, just in case his father was trying to send him a coded message, but the handheld radio only picked up Finnish stations.

Now he sat on the edge of his uncomfortable bed, pop music playing in the background and an English-language book cracked open beside him. He was trying to decide whether it would be more fascinating to have a drink of water or a carton of fruit juice, when a knock sounded at the door and Victor came in.

"Water or juice?" Ruben asked.

"Not for me, thanks." Victor wore his ugly furry

coat over nice, neat trousers. The wind had disordered his hair, blowing it into a straggling halo around his head; his cheeks were flushed and he looked pleased with himself.

"I wasn't offering you a drink. I was... Forget it." Ruben scuffed his feet over the floorboards and sighed. "You're early."

"I've got permission to take you outside." Victor bounced a little and grinned.

"Seriously?" The prospect of getting out of this dump galvanized Ruben into movement. He jumped off the bed and sped around the room, pulling on the black jeans, grey t-shirt and grey sweater Victor had bought for him.

"I wish you'd consider underwear," Victor said, sounding fretful.

"I did consider it, then I decided not to bother." Ruben found two stray socks and sat on the floor to pull on a new pair of ankle boots. "You never know when I might need to be ready for action."

Victor tutted and turned away, but not before Ruben had caught his smile. Pleased that some sort of progress was being made, Ruben stood and wrapped himself in a heavy oilskin jacket. He headed for the door, impatient to be on his way. "Where are we going?"

Victor laughed. "I told you. Outside."

Ruben's sense of excited anticipation lasted approximately thirty seconds. When they were halfway down the stairs, Victor revealed that by 'outside', he didn't mean 'going into the nearest urban center and visiting cafes and bars in search of pretty blond boys'. He didn't even mean 'going to the shops and buying porn'. By 'outside', he simply meant 'going out of doors and walking in the garden'.

The disappointment almost crushed him, but Ruben persevered. He struggled with the huge iron latch on the front door and stepped out into the crisp, cold winter air. Ice crunched beneath his feet, and a fresh fall of snow covered the stone beasts placed either side of the entrance.

"Well!" His breath puffed out in front of him. "If I can't buy porn and I can't flirt with pretty blonds, I guess you'll have to do."

Victor shot him a stern glance.

"Yeah." Ruben grinned. "I love it when you chastise me, even when you do it silently with those killer looks."

An almost-smile tugged at Victor's lips before he got himself under control. "Don't you ever stop?"

"Nope."

Victor heaved a long-suffering sigh and indicated a narrow path swept clear of snow. "This way. There's a walled garden—you can see it from your window..."

Ruben rolled his eyes at the prospect of a close-up look at dead fruit trees, but followed Victor onto the path and around the side of the building. He darted a few quick glances at the safe house, checking for drain pipes and crawling ivy just in case he could escape using those methods, but there was no obvious way out.

His mind raced as he did a slow survey of the garden. Now he was close to them, the walls didn't seem that tall and were full of crumbling brick, ideal for hand and footholds. The copse of black trees also had potential. If he could get out of his room, he might be able to make his escape from this boring hellhole after all. He moved closer to Victor and remarked casually, "If I had my wings, I'd be able to fly right out of here."

Victor shook his head, the action making a strand of hair whip across his face. "You wouldn't get far. The perimeter is monitored by radar, motion sensors, and EMP cross-beams. Launch yourself at that and you'll fry. Even if you tried to run or crawl out of here, the effect would be the same: toasted angel."

Disgruntled, Ruben aimed a kick at the pile of snow lining the path. He told himself he hadn't really wanted to escape anyway. Even if he managed to get out of his room and out of this garden, he still had no idea where he was or how to get back home. No, he was stuck here until he cooperated... or until his father sent someone to rescue him. What a drag.

He lifted his head as another thought occurred to him. "No cameras out here, though? No hidden tape recorders? Not unless you're carrying one."

"I'm not."

They left the main path and trod through squeaky, slip-sliding snow towards the fruit trees. "Apple and plum," Victor said, though how he could tell Ruben had no idea. The trees looked dead to him, stark and black against the snow and the redbrick wall. He pushed against one of the branches, testing it, then clambered up into the tree.

"Be careful!" Victor stood beneath him, concern in his eyes as he looked up.

Ruben grinned. "I'm five feet off the ground and there's about a foot of snow to break my fall. I'm perfectly all right. You, on the other hand..." He balanced on one wide limb and reached up to shake the smaller branches above him. Snow cascaded down, dusting Victor with white. Ruben chuckled and leaned over to shake another set of branches, hooking his arms and legs around the tree limbs. He looked down at Victor, who'd yelped with surprise at the first snow shower and who now stood and laughed as he batted snow from his hair.

Still laughing, Victor glanced up. With glittering snow crystals clinging to his hair, his cheeks flushed pink with cold and his eyes shining with delight, he looked utterly gorgeous.

Ruben froze, his heart suddenly seeming to stop and then to start beating again just a little faster than before. He swallowed, his laughter fading, and stared down at Victor in confusion and wonder.

"What?" Suddenly self-conscious, Victor wrinkled his nose and ruffled his hair, brushing off the melting snow crystals.

"Nothing." Ruben settled onto a low branch close to the trunk and swung his legs back and forth. "You brought me out here for a reason."

"I thought you'd like some fresh air." Victor's gaze skittered away as he spoke.

"You are so bad at telling lies." Ruben waited a moment. "Come on, what is it?"

Victor stepped back and shoved his hands into his coat pockets, the gesture somehow defensive. "Okay, I brought you out here because there are no recording devices. It's just the two of us..."

"Oh, buttercup, are you going to proposition me?"

Victor continued as if Ruben hadn't interrupted. "I just want you to answer my questions without anyone else listening in all the damn time. How much of an active role did you take in your father's coffee business? Why did—"

Ruben scowled. "I'm not in the mood for this."

Taking hold of a branch above him, he swung himself out of the tree. For a split-second while he was in the air, he felt his wing stumps flex involuntarily beneath the layers of the t-shirt and sweater. The action made him catch his breath, his body twisting in automatic response as if to compensate for the beating of his wings.

But he had no wings, and like a stone he dropped the short distance to the ground, landing awkwardly on his knees.

"Ruben!" Victor hurried towards him, compassion and concern on his face. "Are you all right?"

"Fine. I'm fine." Ruben shoved himself upright, furious at his lapse. His knees ached from the sharp shock of the cold and the hard ground, but it was nothing compared to his sense of loss. Trapped in a room for the last few days, he'd managed to push aside the knowledge of his ruined wings. Now he'd been reminded of what he was missing, and the cruelty of his situation hit him with full, vicious anguish. He forced back the hot tears of self-pity blurring his vision, lifted his chin, and strode across the snowy garden towards the trees.

He didn't care where he went, as long as it was away from Victor. He couldn't cope with Victor's kindness or his questions or anything else. He just wanted to be alone.

"Please, Ruben." Clumsy footfalls sounded behind him, Victor's breathing harsh in the still air, and then

Victor put a hand on his arm and tried to pull him around. "I'll give you the feather if you answer my questions."

Ruben turned to face him, wondering if he dared to hope. Victor would give him the feather, he knew that—but what good was it when he didn't know the words of the fucking spell? Schooling his expression into blankness, he said, "Not good enough."

"Then what is?" Victor looked frustrated and miserable. "Elias..."

Shaking his head, Ruben continued onwards. Victor followed, and soon they were away from the garden and into the trees. Snow shivered from dead bracken, and their feet squelched and slid through ice and iron-hard rutted mud. Rotten branches cracked, and the wind hissed through the trees. The air became tense and silent, with the only sounds those made by their passing as they ventured further into the woods.

At length Ruben came to a halt in a small clearing beside a fallen tree. He brushed off the snow and felt the springy green moss with his fingertips. The scent of slumbering growth and the slow rotting of wood filled his nose, and he breathed it in. It was a cold scent, unfamiliar and strange, so he turned to Victor, glad of his lighter, sunnier fragrance. Ruben wanted more, wanted heat and sex and comfort. He wouldn't get that in this chilly place. Unhappiness overwhelmed him again, and he sat down on the tree trunk with a thud.

Victor stood in front of him, not meeting his gaze. He played his foot through the snow at the bottom of the fallen tree, smoothing it out over and over. His shoulders were rounded, his posture despondent. Finally he said, "They're sending me back to England."

Startled, Ruben jerked his head up. "Why?"

"Because their plan didn't work. You're not talking to me." Bitterness crept into Victor's voice. He moved his foot faster through the snow. "I'm a trained interrogator, one of the best... and yet I can't get anything from you."

Ruben blew out a breath and slid backwards over the curve of the tree trunk. "That's because you're approaching this all wrong. Sleep with me and I'll tell you everything. Give me your gorgeous body for one night and I'll spill every FIA secret all over you. Let me love you and I'll give you the world."

It was Victor's turn to stare. "It can't be that easy."

"Sometimes it is." Ruben tilted his head and offered the quick flash of a grin. "I'm a simple creature. I like warmth and sunlight on water and pretty blond boys. Any combination of these makes me happy." He paused, considering Victor for a moment. "What makes you happy, Officer Bischoff?"

Victor gave a pale smile in response. "I don't know. Maybe if you tell me something useful, I'll be happy."

"I'd have thought the idea of getting out of this horrible wintry country would make you happy." Ruben waited a moment longer, then added, "Or going back home to Radcliffe Camera to be with your lover."

Victor frowned, wariness tingeing his features. "Radcliffe Camera?"

Ruben shrugged. "It was on a spell-cast permission slip in your jacket pocket. I thought it must be the name of your hometown or something. Or maybe your lover's hometown."

A blush warmed Victor's cheeks. "You know I don't have a lover."

"I know nothing of the sort," Ruben retorted. "Just because you got all hot for me the other day, it doesn't mean you don't have a lover waiting for you at home. Maybe five or six lovers."

"I think you're confusing me with yourself." Now Victor sounded annoyed.

Ruben shrugged and adopted a casual air. "Well, soon you won't ever see me again. That makes you happy, yes?"

"No." Victor dropped his gaze and burrowed his chin into the furry collar of his coat. "Never seeing you again is..." He stopped.

"Is what?" Ruben got up from the fallen tree and went closer, his pulse racing as he registered the slight shift in tension between them. Victor had gone very still, his gaze fixed to the ground, but Ruben knew he was waiting. He wondered how far he could push this. Keeping his tone light, Ruben asked, "Are you actually admitting that you like me?"

Victor looked up, his expression desperate, conflicted. "You're the most beautiful thing I've ever seen."

Shock and delight warred inside him. Ruben seized Victor by the shoulders and stared at him, struck by a pang of longing so sharp and hot it hurt. "Then why are you fighting me, when we could both be happy?"

Victor tried to shrug out of his grasp. "It's not about that. I don't want to just have sex with you!"

"What else do you want?"

With an angry sigh, Victor shook his head, the sun-striped wings of hair obscuring his expression as he turned away. "This is so unprofessional. I'm sorry. Personal feelings have no place here."

Ruben wasn't going to let him go. Not after that admission. Not until he had a proper answer. Not until he knew beyond doubt what Victor was saying to him in such a half-assed and stumbling way.

"Listen to me, buttercup—your department wants you to fuck me. I want you to fuck me—or at least I want to fuck you, but I'm good with either way—and by your own admission you want it, too! Why are we still standing here in the snow when we could be tucked up warm in bed screwing each other's brains out?"

Victor wrenched himself free, his hands slashing through the air as he punctuated his heartfelt cry: "Because I don't want to end up like them—your other lovers, your pretty little blond boys, the angels and humans..." He broke off, his expression horrified.

Smug warmth radiated through Ruben, and he gave a pleased purr. This sort of reaction he could understand. In recent years, plenty of pretty blond boys had competed for his attention and shown possessive streaks, and he'd always found it very flattering. But he knew Victor wasn't like his usual boys and would therefore need some reassurance.

Ruben had never had to reassure a playmate before and wasn't sure what to say, so he said the first thing that came to mind: "I haven't had a demon as a lover. You'll always be my first."

"That's not what I want. It's not—" Victor's expression sparked with anger and frustration. With a cry of defeat he spun away, but Ruben grabbed him and hauled him back into his arms.

"No," Ruben bit out, "no, you fucking don't," and kissed him.

Victor stood frozen in the embrace for a heartbeat

before he gave a muffled groan and responded, pressing closer, twining ever nearer, his arms going around Ruben's neck and his mouth opening to the kiss.

Ruben slid his hands beneath the long hem of the ugly coat and cupped Victor's arse. It filled his palms perfectly, and Ruben groaned. He backed Victor towards the fallen tree, vaguely thinking they could lie down on it, but then he had a better idea. Breaking the kiss, he unbuttoned his oilskin jacket and yanked it off, then spread it on the snowy ground.

"You'll get cold," Victor protested, though he made no complaint when Ruben drew him down.

"I'm an angel. Our body temperatures are much warmer than demons' bodies." Ruben fiddled with the zipper on Victor's ugly coat. "Besides, we can keep each other nice and hot."

Victor gave a tight, frustrated laugh and pushed his hands away. "Let me." He tugged at the zip and it unsnapped, burring downwards. Ruben pushed him back, hearing the snow crunch as Victor lay half over Ruben's flannel-lined oilskin and half in the frosted bracken. The furry hood of the ugly coat framed his face, blond strands of hair feathering around his cheeks and falling into his eyes. Anticipation shone in his gaze.

Ruben shoved at the unzipped sides of the ugly coat and ran a hand over Victor's chest. He toyed with the buttons on his shirt, slipping one free of its anchor and sliding a finger beneath to touch warm skin and the roughness of hair. Ruben's cock jumped, his arousal hard and immediate. Shit, why had he started this outdoors in the freezing cold? He wanted Victor spread out naked for him, and the weather at minus twenty wasn't conducive to nudity.

While he considered what to do, he kissed Victor again. The taste of him sang through Ruben's blood, an irresistible sweetness. He'd kissed plenty of good boys and they'd never been this hot. Clearly he'd been wasting his time with humans and other angels. From now on, he'd only fuck demons—though in truth the only demon he wanted to fuck was pinned beneath him. Why would he want a taste of anything else when he had such a glorious, responsive creature in his arms?

Ruben deepened the kiss, feeling Victor arch up against him. Victor raked his hands through Ruben's hair, the gesture both tender and commanding. Ruben smiled, enjoying the spirited flash of dominance. This was what he wanted, what he yearned for—a lover who'd challenge him, who'd intrigue and fascinate him. The fact that it had taken a week to get this far with Victor was a good sign. Most of Ruben's romantic relationships ran their course after four days.

Gentling the embrace, Ruben trailed kisses from Victor's mouth down over his neck, nuzzling at the rapid thrum of his pulse, licking at the delicate taste of his skin.

"Elias, Elias..." Victor sounded stunned, the yearning in his voice something Ruben had never heard before. He tried to recall any of his lovers wanting him with quite so much passion and couldn't name a single one.

"Buttercup." Ruben pulled at the collar of his sensible button-down shirt and bit Victor's pale, vulnerable throat. "God, Victor. Don't stop me this time."

"We mustn't," Victor gasped. "I can't."

His protests didn't sound very convincing. "We must," Ruben murmured, "and you can." He kissed Victor again, a brief possession of his mouth, a swift stab of tongue past yielding lips, then he shifted position and drew back onto his knees, settling astride one of Victor's thighs.

In a matter of seconds he'd unbuckled Victor's belt and pushed up his shirt. Ruben leaned down and rubbed his face over the trail of dark hair, breathing in the scent of Victor's waking desire. He unbuttoned Victor's sensible, boring trousers and caught at the waistband, then dragged down his trousers and his underwear together until the fabric twisted around Victor's knees.

Ruben took a moment to admire the view. He licked his lips at the sight of the hard cock he'd groped so thoroughly a few days ago. Oh, it was even better than he'd imagined, standing proud from the deliciously dark nest of pubic hair. Unable to resist, he dipped his head and inhaled the warm, musky scent of Victor's cock from root to head.

Victor raised his hips in offering, but Ruben wanted to wait, wanted to savor this experience. He contented himself by blowing a stream of air the full length of Victor's shaft, watching him twitch and writhe in response. Grinning, Ruben prepared to nuzzle into the heat of Victor's balls when he saw his tail.

Ruben stared. Just as Victor had said, his tail was wrapped tight around his leg, the skin as smooth, taut, and satiny as his erection. The colour of his tail changed in subtle gradations from the pale tones of his skin through to scarlet at the sharp-pointed tip. As Ruben watched, Victor flexed his tail, the coils tightening further until the flesh of his thigh showed white between each loop of tail.

"Wow," Ruben said. He didn't know what he liked most, Victor's cock or his tail. He wondered if Victor had ever considered using his tail for kinky play, and filed that thought away for later. Ruben lowered himself onto his hands and knees, crouching over Victor's legs as he shuffled to get closer to that fabulous tail. He stroked it with a fingertip, receiving a squeak of response from Victor, then he tried to unravel the tail from its death-grip around Victor's thigh.

"No," Victor said, his voice lacking conviction, but the tail remained firmly wrapped about his leg.

Unwilling to give up just yet, Ruben kissed the coil closest to him. The skin was softer than he expected, his lips gliding over the tail with slick ease. It was all solid muscle, trembling with tension as he kissed and licked his way around as much of the coil as possible. He moved from one loop to the next, working down Victor's thigh towards his knee to where the point of his tail twitched back and forth.

Ruben shoved Victor's underwear down a little further so he could get at the point of his tail. He watched it flick to and fro in tiny increments, then put his mouth on it and sucked the tip into his mouth.

Victor's entire body went stiff. He gasped, holding completely still.

"Is that good?" Ruben glanced up to see Victor's expression warring between delight and shame. "You taste fantastic, buttercup. I want to play with all of your tail."

Apparently unable to speak, Victor shook his head, his hair whipping across his face to hide his blushes.

"Next time, then." Ruben kissed the tip of his tail a final time then mouthed at the flesh of his thigh bisected by each coil. He trailed his tongue up Victor's inner thigh, tickling at the juncture between leg and torso, then purred as he nuzzled at his balls.

He inhaled deeply, filling his head with Victor's scent. Ruben licked his sac, playing the weight of Victor's balls on his tongue, gently tugging at the curls of hair. Victor groaned, his cock leaking pre-cum and his scent thickening. His shaft grew harder, throbbing with heat.

Ruben couldn't wait any longer. "I've wanted to do this from the first time I saw you," he murmured, and took Victor's cock into his mouth.

Victor moaned; a sexy, helpless sound.

Ruben shivered with lust. Victor kept on making those noises, breathy moans and gasps and half-whispered pleadings for more. Ruben reveled in the sound of his name from Victor's lips almost as much as he enjoyed the hard thrust of Victor's cock in his mouth. He sucked, humming with pleasure, deep-throating him and then drawing back up to concentrate on the sensitive underside of the cockhead. Victor's taste and smell surrounded him, each subtle nuance of scent an indication to Ruben of what Victor would like best.

Victor reached out clumsily, his hands grasping through Ruben's hair to hold him in place. He seemed oblivious to the cold in the air and the snow on the ground, lost in the combined heat of their bodies. Ruben stroked his fingertips through the sheen of sweat between Victor's thighs, then rubbed his thumbs beneath his balls, lifting them, toying with them.

A desperate cry escaped Victor. He thrashed and writhed on the coats, his head snapping from side to side, the wings of his hair disordered and trailing strands caught in his open, panting mouth. His body heaved and trembled as he climbed towards orgasm, his muscles tensing as Ruben took him higher.

The taste of pre-cum sharpened on his tongue. Ruben snuffled, his nose pressed to Victor's belly as he indulged in the sensation of strong, hard cock forced between his lips. The smell and taste drove him wild. Ruben gasped, on the brink of tumbling into something he didn't want to name. Victor's scent intoxicated him, managed to inflame his senses yet soothe the lingering anxieties he tried to hide at the back of his mind. Victor smelled of trust and honor and love, a fragrance rich and sweet enough to turn any man's head.

Feeling the change in Victor's tension, Ruben lavished attention on his cockhead then sucked him deep. He heard Victor cry out, felt him clutch tight at his hair, and then the hot gush of spunk filled his mouth.

Ruben swallowed greedily then pulled back, letting some semen dribble between his slack lips so he could chase it with his tongue. Victor bucked and writhed, riding his orgasm to the last drop, and Ruben drank it all down.

Murmuring with satisfaction, Ruben cleaned Victor's cock with lazy flicks of his tongue. Victor could do nothing but lie there, flinching with ticklish reaction and gasping for breath, his eyes closed and an expression of stunned disbelief on his face.

Kneeling over him, Ruben unzipped his trousers and freed his own fierce erection. He grasped his cock, moaning at how hard and hot it felt in his hand, then stroked its length to smear the oozing wetness from the tip over his palm. Taking a firm hold, he started to jerk off, his movements fast and decisive.

He knew it wouldn't take long. Ruben stared at Victor the whole time, taking in the sight of his sprawled, partially clothed body, then gazing at his mouth, imagining Victor going down on him, imagining those soft, pouting lips stretched wide around his cock. Ruben's breath caught and he felt his wing stumps twitch, felt the hot, twisting tremor of climax begin at the base of his spine.

"Victor," he gasped, and their gazes met. The tender, wondering look in Victor's eyes undid him, and Ruben came, his seed splashing in thick white trails over Victor's belly and thighs.

Ruben dropped his hand and hung over Victor, his heart thundering, his breath shuddering out of him in short, sharp bursts. Pleasure rolled through him, buzzing his head. He couldn't feel anything else but ecstasy; didn't know anything else but Victor lying beneath him.

After a while Ruben tucked himself away, cleaned up the spill of his semen from Victor's body, and adjusted his clothing. With a deep sigh, Ruben settled on top of his new demon lover, warming him against the cold. He smiled and nuzzled through Victor's hair, enjoying the sense of peace and completion. "I knew you'd be a great lay," he murmured, dropping a kiss on Victor's jaw. "Knew it from the moment you walked into my room."

Victor shifted beneath him, seeming to come back to earth with a thud. "No."

"No?" Puzzled, Ruben lifted himself up onto his elbows and looked down.

"No. Get off." Victor wouldn't meet his gaze. His breathing accelerated, becoming sharp and panicked. He seemed embarrassed about what they'd done. When Ruben didn't move, Victor shoved at him. "Get the Hell off me!"

"What's wrong?"

"This. This is wrong." Victor wriggled out from beneath him and put his clothes in order, his face flaming. "Please don't say anything. It shouldn't have happened. I—I'm sorry, so sorry..."

Still apologizing, his voice high and taut with anxiety, Victor drew up the zip on his coat and stumbled backwards. His gaze jumped over Ruben, his eyes wide with regret and shame. "I've ruined everything. This is a disaster. I can't—"

Without finishing his sentence, he started to hurry away, shambling like a drunk.

Utterly bewildered, Ruben shook his head and climbed to his feet, almost tripping over his oilskin lying on the snow. "Don't leave. Don't leave me." When Victor didn't even pause, Ruben tried to think of some way to bring him back. He called out: "Before I fell, there was a plane crash."

Victor stopped. Slowly he turned. "What?"

"That's the last thing I remember. A plane crash." Ruben put a hand to his head, the memory still so vivid. His wing stumps flexed a little, a dull echo of pain scratching at him. "I was accompanying the flight to Spain when we ran into an electrical storm somewhere around latitude 16°N, longitude 24°W."

His expression clearing, Victor ventured back towards him. Despite his obvious curiosity, he kept a wary distance. "Why were you accompanying the plane?"

Ruben exhaled. He was tired of concealing the truth. "A friend of a friend was travelling on board. My friend wanted to be sure his friend arrived safely."

Victor took a step closer. "What's his name?"

"My friend? Marc Soto. The FIA's Rio Resident." Ruben gave a weary smile. "And his friend is a human. Valentin Tristan."

CHAPTER 7

Victor slammed the heavy front door behind him and leaned against it for a moment, his heart hammering and his emotions twisted up inside him. Oh God, he could still feel Ruben's mouth on his cock, the long, slow strokes of his tongue over his tail... Victor moaned aloud, the sound echoing in the empty hallway. He had to stop this, had to regain his self-control.

He pushed himself from the door and straightened up, brushing his hands through his hair. Damp leaves and twigs had matted into the strands at the back and he tugged them out with a furious gesture. How could he have been so stupid, so weak?

It was useless to deny his attraction to Ruben. He'd never wanted anyone like this before. His previous relationships had been safe, controlled—fun, but good-mannered and appropriate fun. None of his former boyfriends would have ever considered being intimate outside of the bedroom. That was just how things worked.

And now there was Ruben. His interrogation subject. A prisoner of the DTM. An angel. Absolutely forbidden to him in every way, despite what his orders stated.

Victor rubbed a hand across his face. It wasn't just that Ruben was an angel, though that had played a big part in it. It was more the fact that he'd started looking forward to the interrogations. He liked seeing Ruben in the clothes he'd picked out in Stockmann's. He liked listening to Ruben's evasive answers to the standard questions, and his unguarded conversations about his yacht, or sailing around the Mediterranean, or his favorite holiday spots... Even if he wasn't sharing top-level FIA secrets, Ruben's words conjured longing in Victor. Not a longing to experience these fabled delights, but a longing to know more about Ruben.

He recognized the bravado that overlay a deep insecurity. Several times he'd wanted to dig deeper, to tell Ruben he knew why he was hiding behind his playboy mask, but this wasn't the time or place to do it. All he could do was keep asking the questions and try to find a new angle of attack, and hope Ruben would start giving him answers.

But he hadn't wanted to get the answers like this. Disgust rose in his throat like nausea as Victor imagined what Ruben must think of him now. He hoped Ruben didn't believe he'd allowed the blowjob for the sole purpose of gaining information. The idea made him sick. He didn't want to be known as someone who'd slept his way up the career ladder, even if he'd been ordered to do it. He'd always wanted to be seen as someone respectable and good at his job, someone loyal and trustworthy and untainted by scandal despite his father's reputation.

But now, because of Ruben, because of his lack of control, all that was shot to Hell. Victor felt his ambitions tumble around him and melt like fresh-fallen snow.

"Enough," he told himself, his voice harsh. He yanked at the zip on his coat and shrugged out of it, then hung it on the coat-rack in the hall. Banishing his anxieties, he strode to the foot of the staircase and checked the small black-and-white monitors that showed external views of the garden.

Ruben was sitting on a bench beside the empty fountain in the front garden, his head bowed and his shoulders hunched against the cold of the day. Victor hesitated, wanting to go back to him, but he set his jaw and turned away. Ruben would be safe enough outside. There was no way he could escape.

Victor climbed the stairs and pushed open the door to the general office. Emil and two other demon operations specialists were gathered around a monitor, commenting on what they were watching with low voices and throaty laughter. They seemed so absorbed that they didn't hear him when he entered the room. Curious, Victor remained silent as he went towards them.

A second later, he glimpsed what was on the screen and felt his heart stop with horrified shock. His colleagues were watching the playback of Ruben giving him a blowjob.

Victor stood frozen, unable to tear his gaze away from the monitor. The shot was fuzzy, sometimes out of focus, and had clearly been taken long-range, but it was enough to pick up the detail of what they were doing. Mercifully there was no accompanying soundtrack, but Victor remembered every last gasp and moan, every rustle of clothing and every slick, wet sound of mouths against skin.

He watched himself fist his hands into Ruben's hair, dragging him closer. He registered the intense expression of pleasure on his face as he turned his head to one side, and saw Ruben's delighted smile before he took another mouthful. Victor's cock stirred in response, and he made a strangled sound as he tried to quash the unwelcome kick of lust.

"Officer Bischoff!" His colleagues jumped and faced him, embarrassment and guilt on every expression. One of them pressed a button, closing the playback feed, and the screen went blank except for a pulsing cursor.

Mortified, Victor stared at them. He couldn't let them know how humiliated he felt. Instead he forced steel into his voice and said sharply, "When you've all finished wanking off over me doing my job, perhaps you could do your jobs and run a check on a human called Valentin Tristan."

Without waiting for a reaction, he strode over to a nearby terminal and sat down at it, then began opening the access port to his log-in protocols on the Oxford system. "While you lot waste time, I'm going to look for plane crash reports within the FIA."

"Plane crash?" Emil came over to join him, signaling to the other demons to get on with their work.

Victor ignored him as the Oxford screens popped up and prompted him for his passwords. Soon he was into the familiar layout of his desktop display and called up the crash, malfunction, and forced landing data reports from the last ten days. At the same time, he ran the coordinates Ruben had given him. Information slowly loaded on the screen, and he murmured, "The Cape Verde Islands."

Emil perched on the desk next to him. "What's this about?"

Victor didn't look up, too engrossed in reading the scrolling data reports. "Ruben—Barbosa Minor—just told me he was accompanying a flight from Rio to Spain. He thinks the plane crashed in an electrical storm... and whatever caused the crash was also responsible for sending him here."

"So he's finally decided to talk." Emil gave a dirty laugh. "What did I tell you? Wired for sex, that one.

All you had to do was give him what he wanted and he's putty in your hands. I bet we'll get much more out of him now."

Victor swallowed his anger, his fingernails digging into his palms. "It won't happen again."

Tilting his head, Emil stared at him with open curiosity. "Why not? You seemed to enjoy it."

"Sleeping with a subject is a huge mistake."

"Only if you develop feelings for him." Emil leaned closer and lowered his voice. "You're not going to be stupid enough to fall for Barbosa Minor, are you, Officer Bischoff?"

"Of course not." Victor gritted his teeth and hoped he wasn't blushing. The anger rose in him again, and he thumped the side of the monitor when the text-scrolling went even slower. "This damn machine! It's so outdated."

Emil sniffed. "Like everything else in life, you just need to know how to handle it the right way." He slid from the desk and pulled up a chair from a nearby workstation. Propping his chin in his hands, he watched as Victor jotted a few notes on a yellow legal pad and clicked on various reports.

"Nothing. There's nothing here." Victor hated people hovering over him while he worked, especially when he was engaged in what was turning out to be a fruitless search. Had Ruben lied to him or misled him about the crash or about the coordinates? He checked again. Flights from Rio to the south and east of Spain passed over the Cape Verde Islands, but there was nothing on any of the intercepted reports about a crash or forced landing. There wasn't even a log of any aircraft malfunction, which would be routine if a plane had been damaged in an electrical storm.

"Let me look." Emil nudged closer.

Victor logged out and stood, pacing towards the window. He stared through the misted glass at the front garden. Ruben must have come inside by now. Victor followed the track of his footprints around the fountain and across the lawns and back onto the path leading to the door. Ruben hadn't lied to him. He wouldn't. Victor knew he'd been speaking the truth. But what the Hell had happened to that plane? And how had Ruben got from the Cape Verde Islands to southern Finland? No mere electrical storm could have done that.

He turned over the idea of Joseph Cabrera's involvement again. Whoever had done this had organized it with skill and cunning. It was impossible to search for magic and power surges during an electrical storm, which suggested that the person—or angel—behind this plan had access to weather reports as well as a great deal of magic to spell-cast Ruben from one place to the other without actually killing him outright.

Unless whoever was behind this had wanted Ruben dead, and they'd miscalculated.

Victor went cold. Fear gripped his heart and he forced back the knot of anxiety lodged in his throat. Turning, he strode over to Emil and curled his hands around the side of his chair. "Has there been any chatter on the wires about Barbosa Minor's disappearance?"

One of the other demons answered. "There was a report in the teen celebrity magazine Atrevida that Barbosa Minor hooked up with a stunning blond hunk and is doing the horizontal samba with him in Sardinia." The demon gave a salacious grin. "Guess they got it right apart from the location, huh?"

Victor gave him a freezing look of contempt. "Atrevida? What the Hell?"

"Barbosa Minor often graces its august pages," Emil said. "He even made the cover a few times. Your new lover is considered quite the catch in the FIA."

"He's not my..." Victor stopped himself, unwilling to give them the satisfaction of his feeble denials. "Widen the search criteria. Check the records of any plane leaving from Rio de Janeiro in the past ten days or so."

The demon muttered but tapped at the computer. "Nothing."

"There must be something." Victor folded his arms as he paced back and forth. "What about

Valentin Tristan? Have you tracked down his details yet?"

"I'm looking," Emil said, "and there's nothing here, either."

"You're not looking hard enough." Victor leaned over Emil's shoulder at the screen, which listed files in Finnish and English. In the search box, he typed 'Valentin Tristan' and came up with a blank query page and the prompt to try again.

"Told you so," Emil said. "I've tried all permutations of his name and still come up with nothing."

"Let's do it this way, then." Victor pushed Emil out of the way and called up the FIA personnel files, searching through the 'S' category individually. Then, on a whim, he pulled up the records for the DTM personnel and did the same thing. Still nothing. Reluctant to abandon the hunt, Victor searched through the 'deleted personnel' folders. It was a long shot, but it paid off.

A page loaded onto the screen. A photograph of a smiling, dark-haired human emerged, but the usual information on education, work history, and family background had been repressed.

Victor frowned. "He's here, in the deleted personnel."

Emil rolled his chair closer. "He's dead?"

"I don't know. This doesn't make any sense." Victor moved the cursor down the page. "There's a link to another file."

"A file I don't have the authority to access." Emil pulled the keyboard towards him as a blank screen loaded. He tapped in a series of departmental codes, but each time the screen flashed up the message in two languages: Access Denied.

"Let me try again." Victor nudged Emil out of the way and sat in the chair, shifting it closer to the desk. He flexed his fingers then began entering a series of binary numbers. "I was pretty good at systems-wide code-breaking in training college."

"Code-breaking?" Emil sounded shocked. "You're trying to hack the central DTM mainframe! We're working for them, remember?"

"And they're hiding information from us. The end justifies the means."

"Not when they sack us for breaking into their system!"

Victor pushed the hair from his eyes and grinned up at Emil. "Don't watch, then. Make me a cup of coffee."

Still muttering, Emil retreated to the kitchen cubicle. Another five minutes and he returned, a mug of coffee between his hands. "Here. How's it going?"

"Good." Victor snagged the mug and brought it to his lips, sipping at the scalding liquid. He made a noise of pleasure as the caffeine unraveled inside him, sharpening his senses. "I've managed to get through two more levels."

"Learned anything useful?"

Victor put down his coffee. "Not really. I've got Valentin's education records and there's some bank transactions here that seem a bit strange—the financial trail goes in and out of several Swiss banks but the originator is hidden..." Entering another set of numbers, Victor sat back and waited. He glanced at Emil. "You'd think if he was being paid by the FIA, there'd be a traceable account."

"This is the FIA we're talking about." Emil grimaced. "Nothing they do is logical."

With a sigh, Victor reached for his coffee again. His enthusiasm for this project was running thin. The screen flashed, and Victor looked at the scrolling information. His hands tightened around the mug as he read, and when he spoke, he heard the uncertainty crack his voice. "He's a scientist. A caffeine scientist."

"What?" Emil leaned across to look at the screen. "What do you mean?"

Victor took a deep breath. "Valentin Tristan was a DTM human. He defected to the FIA five years ago when he was on staff at our embassy in Monaco."

A moment of silence rippled out around them.

Emil cleared his throat. "Monaco was in the hands of the angels back then. They barely tolerated DTM presence in the embassy. Who was the Resident at the time? He must have known something about the defection."

Victor swallowed. "It was my father."

Another silence, and then Emil turned to stare at him, his expression stunned. "Shit. No wonder this has a high-level clearance."

His earlier anger returned, and Victor met Emil's gaze without flinching. "You told me my father wasn't being investigated."

Emil backed away, his hands held up in a placatory gesture. "I don't know if he is or not! I'm only a third rank demon, like you. They tell me nothing except on a need-to-know basis. I just do as I'm told."

"Well, I need to know." Victor shoved aside his mug, heedless of the hot coffee that slopped onto the desk. He entered more numbers, determined to pull the entire file out of the bowels of the mainframe. "My dad's innocent. He would never assist with a defection."

"Are you sure?" Emil asked softly.

Victor set his jaw. He wasn't sure, and that was the

problem. As far as his father was concerned, he couldn't be sure of anything.

"He's innocent," Victor said, injecting certainty into his tone. "I know he is."

A second later, a red screen flashed up and the computer started beeping. Unauthorised access detected. System rebooting. Shutting down in 5, 4, 3, 2, 1...

"Shit." Victor took his hands from the keyboard. "I almost had it."

"You triggered a system-wide shutdown." Emil stared at him in horror. "They know you hacked into their files."

Victor blew out a breath. "Relax. It doesn't matter."

"Doesn't matter?" Emil almost screeched. "You hacked the DTM mainframe using my log-in!"

CHAPTER 8

Ruben sat on the table in his room, swinging his legs back and forth as he waited for his daily interrogation. Something had changed within the building since yesterday—people were creeping around and speaking in hushed whispers. Earlier that morning, the human who brought Ruben his breakfast had scuttled in and out of the room without so much as a single word of greeting.

Puzzled by this behaviour, as the human usually spoke at least four words to him, Ruben had opened the window and leaned out to eavesdrop on the conversation of a couple of demons who regularly went for a cigarette break just beneath his room. From their muted chatter, he discovered that Victor was in some sort of trouble with DTM officials.

Ruben hoped it wasn't because of what they'd done yesterday. He wriggled just at the thought of it—Victor's lithe, sexy tail and his hard, sexy cock, and those sexy, sexy noises he made just before he came, and...

With a groan, Ruben forced himself to think of something else. Victor had stolen every last ounce of common sense from him. The way he'd run off afterwards had almost broken Ruben's heart. He wasn't accustomed to feeling bad about anything, so yesterday when a dull, nagging ache took up residence in his chest, Ruben decided it was indigestion before he remembered the only thing he'd eaten all day was Officer Bischoff.

Footsteps in the corridor outside made Ruben perk up at the idea of a distraction. Good, he didn't want to wallow in all this soul-searching crap. His wing stumps twitched and he sat forward on the edge of the table as the lock clicked and the door opened.

Officer Olsen came into the room, his expression set like concrete. He held a clipboard and a dossier in his hands, and as he approached the table, he looked at Ruben's bare feet and unbuttoned shirt with a grimace of distaste.

"Sit down, please." Olsen indicated the chair opposite.

Ruben refused to move. "Where's Victor?"

Olsen placed his things on the table and seated himself. "Sit down, Barbosa."

"Not until you tell me where Victor is." Bristling

with dislike, Ruben tucked one foot beneath him and lounged on the table. He smiled inwardly when Olsen flinched, but it was a short-lived victory.

"Officer Bischoff is out of the office today."

Ruben slid lower on the desk and gave the pale demon a dazzling, seductive smile. "Where is he?"

Olsen swallowed, blushed, and dropped his gaze. A moment later he had himself under control and gave Ruben a bland look. "Officer Bischoff has been removed from the premises due to his misconduct yesterday."

"Misconduct?" Ruben sat up straight, his wing stumps vibrating with tension.

"Nothing to do with you, Barbosa." Olsen's voice was clipped. He sorted through his notes and uncapped a pen. "Now then, yesterday you told Officer Bischoff about a plane crash at a pair of coordinates pinpointing the Cape Verde Islands. We have combed through all available data from both the DTM and FIA, and let me tell you, Barbosa Minor, there is no record of a plane crash at that location."

"There must be."

Olsen gave him a chilly smile. "I assure you, there isn't."

Ruben gritted his teeth. "I know what I saw."

Silence fell between them, and then Olsen leaned forward. "Perhaps you were mistaken. Perhaps," he continued as Ruben opened his mouth to protest, "you could be persuaded to give us the right coordinates of the crash site..."

Cold dread tickled Ruben's insides. The expression froze on his face and his heartbeat gave a stuttering thud. He knew it—he just fucking knew it. Those bastard demons had been planning this the whole time. Soften him up with the pretty blond and then bring on the creepy torture guys.

Ruben had seen his father torturing FIA dissidents. Angel, demon or human, it made no matter to Barbosa Senior—he treated them all the same. The memory of the horrors he'd witnessed made Ruben break out into a sweat. He turned his head away, unable to bear the scent of his own fear.

"Persuaded," he said, keeping his voice steady. "How?"

"Well..." Olsen fiddled with his fountain pen. "How about this, for starters?" From his jacket he took a plastic pass and slid it across the table.

Ruben stared. "What the Hell is that?"

"A pass," Olsen said as if he were simple. "A city-wide pass for Turku. It permits you to leave the quarantine of the safe house and move freely around the city."

"You'll let me out?" Ruben could hardly believe it. "On my own?"

Olsen gave him a patronizing look. "One of our demons will tail you at a discreet distance, of course. Just for your own safety, you understand. But you'll be allowed to go wherever you wish within Turku city limits."

Ruben picked up the pass and examined it. "Can I go clubbing?"

Now Olsen looked pained. "I suppose..."

"And if I hook up with a pretty blond—what will your demon guy do then? Watch us? Join in?"

Olsen spluttered, his face turning crimson.

"I don't mind—I'm quite into voyeurism and threesomes," Ruben continued happily, tucking the pass into his jeans pocket, "but I like to know in advance if there's going to be someone official getting down with me, you know?"

"I—I..." Olsen seemed on the verge of apoplexy.

Ruben sighed and jumped off the table. Somehow it wasn't as much fun teasing Officer Olsen. Victor was much more responsive and a whole lot hotter.

"In exchange for the pass, we want information!" Olsen managed to squawk.

"You have it already." Ruben buttoned his shirt and looked around for a pair of socks. "Cape Verde Islands. Valentin Tristan. Marc Soto. Coffee. Do I have to spell it out for you or what?"

Olsen made a despairing noise and clutched at his head. "Please! I'm authorized to give you spending money—five hundred euro in used notes—it's in your coat pocket downstairs. I can get you a chauffeur-driven car to take you around Turku. I can even get you a guide to the best nightspots and porn shops... but please tell me the truth about the plane crash and how you ended up here!"

Wriggling his feet into his new shoes, Ruben turned. "There's only one thing I want from this godforsaken place."

Relief washed across Olsen's face. "What is it?"

"I want Officer Victor Bischoff."

The relief turned to irritation. "He's not here."

Ruben took a step forward. "I want him warm, willing, and naked in my bed."

A blush rose to Olsen's cheeks. "That's impossible. I told you. He's not here. He's been taken off the case."

"I won't talk to anyone else." Ruben narrowed his gaze. "Give me Officer Bischoff—now."

For a moment, Olsen mumbled and scribbled something in his notes, then he collected his stuff together and stood. "It would be better for everybody if you talked to me," he said, his expression apologetic.

Ruben folded his arms. "Victor. Here. Now."

"Okay, okay! I'll see what I can do." Olsen flushed, a sheen of sweat on his upper lip. "It's against orders, but if it's the only way... I'll go and find him. Stay here. You're not permitted to leave the premises until I come back."

Olsen left the room clutching his notes and dossier, still babbling to himself. Ruben waited until he heard the lock click shut before he sighed and went to the window. Five minutes later, he saw Olsen and a couple of his demon buddies hurry out onto the wide graveled driveway, heading for their cars. All three tore away at high speed, leaving Ruben both amused and irritated.

He wondered if Victor had been sent back to Radcliffe Camera already, or if he was in Helsinki. He had no idea how far Turku was from Helsinki, but he was sure it wasn't just down the road. Not that it mattered, Ruben thought—Officer Olsen and his pals were out of his hair for a while.

He sprawled on the bed, scuffing his shoes across the quilt deliberately. They hated it when he did that. Then he put his hands behind his head while he considered what to do with his free time. Fantasizing about Victor was always fun. Jerking off while fantasizing about Victor was even better. But for some reason, he wasn't in the mood. His irritation at Olsen turned to irritation at himself, and Ruben curled up into a ball, feeling despair and misery creeping up on him.

He pressed the heel of his hand to his forehead. How the fuck was he going to get out of here? It had been over a week now and he'd heard nothing, sensed nothing. He knew his father was more than powerful enough to pierce the DTM's crappy defenses, even if it was only momentary, even if only to tell Ruben how to break out of this dump—and yet his father didn't come.

Ruben rolled onto his front and punched the pillow. Sure, it was an understatement to say that he and his father didn't get on very well, but still, there was no way Ruben Barbosa Senior would let his son and heir rot in a freezing cold hellhole in Finland.

Or maybe he would. Ruben sighed and turned onto his side as he considered the possibility. Yeah, his father was probably trying to teach him a lesson. He'd been really pissed off about Ruben and his last boyfriend appearing on the covers of half a dozen gossip magazines. Not even the Barbosa wealth had been enough to force the magazines to pull the images, which featured Ruben and the blond—what the Hell was his name again? Ruben couldn't remember—in a naked X-rated embrace on the deck of his yacht.

Ruben smiled. He couldn't remember the blond's name but he remembered with glee his father's fury. Barbosa Senior had been so angry he'd hurled an antique coffee pot at Ruben's head. He'd ducked, the pot had hit the wall and smashed to pieces, and hot coffee had splattered across a priceless Persian carpet. Good times—and a very good reason for his protracted stay in this benighted snowy country.

The sound of a car engine outside made Ruben roll off the bed and go back to the window. A silver Mercedes had pulled up, and as Ruben watched, two men got out. They didn't speak to one another, but walked purposefully towards the front entrance.

Ruben frowned. One of them looked a little familiar, but he must have been mistaken. He remained by the window for a while then turned when he heard the snap of the lock. The two men came into his room, and Ruben stared in astonishment. "Raul? Raul Soler?"

Raul gave him a brief, businesslike smile. "Hello, Ruben."

"But—but... you're dead!" Ruben didn't know whether to shrink back against the wall or go closer. His gaze went to the other man, paler than Victor and with icy blue eyes and blond hair worn long enough for it to curl at the ends. Ruben's instinctive response to blonds was tempered by the expression of utter boredom on the man's face.

He looked back at Raul. "My father told me you

died on your last mission. The one in Switzerland. I even went to your funeral!"

Raul exchanged a glance with the bored blond.

"What's going on? And who the Hell is he? Can't he talk?" Ruben was beginning to feel freaked out. The last time he'd seen Raul had been two years ago at a party held at the Barbosa residence. Though they'd never been close friends, they moved in the same circles, and Ruben had been honestly sad when he'd heard the news of Raul's death. And yet here he was, alive and well.

"I'm glad you're not dead," Ruben said. "Is this a social call?"

The bored blond rolled his eyes. "It's a rescue."

"Oh, you do talk." Ruben stared at him. "And you are...?"

"Isaac Bertram. Ex-officer in the DTM. The subject I targeted in Switzerland." Raul smiled again, warmer this time. "My lover. The demon I gave up my wings for."

"Gave up your wings?" Ruben sat down on his bed, shock making him weak for a moment. He hadn't realised it until now, but that was what was different about Raul—no wings, not even tucked up small and flat. No glimmer of magic. Nothing about him suggested he'd ever been an angel. His voice cracking, Ruben asked, "You're human?"

"He is. So am I." Isaac strolled around the room. "Get your stuff. We're leaving."

Ruben flapped his hands. "Wait. Just wait a minute. Someone tell me what's going on."

Isaac sighed. "Are you stupid?"

"Don't be so impatient." Raul gave his lover an affectionate look then turned to Ruben. "We're getting you out of here. Your father called me last night with orders to find some way of rescuing you."

"He did?" Somewhat belatedly, Ruben remembered the A/V bugs. He jumped up. "Uh, guys, the demons are recording all this. If we're going, we should go now before someone comes to check."

Isaac huffed. "I was a demon. I worked here—and they haven't changed the codes. The A/V is disabled. Get your things and let's go."

Ruben hurried around the room, shoving his toothbrush and a couple of unread books into a spare shirt. After a moment's hesitation, he pocketed the sleeping tablets. "I'm ready."

Isaac headed for the door, leaving Ruben to follow Raul. "I'll explain things once we're in the car," Raul said.

"Er, great. That would be good." Ruben hurried down the staircase and grabbed his coat, remembering the five hundred euro Officer Olsen had promised him. As he crossed the threshold of the safe house, Ruben paused, a touch of sadness washing over him. If only he'd had the chance to say goodbye to Victor... But that was a stupid thought, and he shoved it to the back of his mind.

Outside, the air was frozen with stillness. The noise of the car doors slamming seemed overly loud, and Ruben squished down on the backseat, waiting for the humans inside the house to come chasing after them. But it seemed that Isaac had been right about his insider knowledge, and no one challenged them as they drove out of the gates and turned onto the road.

Raul wriggled around in his seat so he could look back at Ruben. "We'll take you into the center of Turku, and after that it's up to you."

Ruben sat up straight. "My father didn't give you any other instructions concerning me?"

"Only to get you out of the safe house and drop you in the city center. That's it." Raul shrugged. "You know what he's like."

Isaac snorted and drove a little faster.

They went around a corner and Ruben slid sideways on the leather seats. He grabbed at the door to stop from tipping over. "My father asked you to do this because you wouldn't register as an angel or a demon at the border scans, right? Your scans would show you as human."

"That's right. One of the advantages of being human is that we can sneak across borders with fake passports." Raul gripped the headrest of the front seat as they cornered again. "Isaac, slow down."

"All Finns drive like crazy people," Isaac said. "Stop complaining."

"But... you're human." Ruben couldn't get his head around it. "How did that happen?"

Raul settled against the seat. "I was sent to Switzerland as a sleeper agent. I had to make contact with Isaac and seduce him, then record the details of several high-level banking transactions." He flicked a glance at Isaac, his expression softening slightly. "I didn't expect to lose my wings over it, but then again, I didn't expect to fall in love, either."

Ruben shook his head. "My God."

"I managed to get some of the details the FIA wanted, but then Isaac discovered what I was doing. He informed his DTM superiors, but because we were both in Switzerland, a neutral, non-extradition country, no one could touch us. So we decided to both resign and... Well, we both lost our wings."

"Technically we cannot leave Switzerland," Isaac added. "Both governments have issued warrants for our arrest if ever we leave the country, but Raul insisted on coming here."

Raul patted his arm. "Admit it, you like seeing Finland again."

Isaac made a rude noise. "I would like it better if we weren't in constant danger."

"You won't need to worry about me soon," Ruben said.

"I'm not worrying about you, stupid." Isaac glanced at him in the rear view mirror and Ruben looked away.

As they approached the city, Ruben leaned towards Raul. "Do you know the spell for wing regeneration?"

Raul seemed embarrassed. "It's not so much a spell as a state of mind. You have to visualize your wings growing again... but it's difficult to get right. It'd be easier for you to wait until you were back in FIA territory. All you need then is someone sharing your DNA matrix to give permission for you to use one of their feathers, and you can summon back your wings. But I imagine your father will just spell-cast them for you."

Isaac snorted again.

Giving his lover an uneasy glance, Raul continued, "There is another way, though I don't know how reliable the method is."

"What is it?"

Raul twisted in his seat again to face Ruben. "You need to have sex with a demon on a ley line, take the demonic energy from their orgasm, and that will restore your wings."

Ruben brightened. That seemed a much more appealing option than going home and waiting for his father to get round to regenerating his wings. "Sounds great. Where's the nearest ley line?"

Isaac laughed. "First you need a willing demon."

"That's not an issue." Puffing himself up, Ruben brushed a hand through his hair and preened. "I'm hot. I can pull any demon I want."

"Yeah, right." Isaac sounded unimpressed. "And they'll sling your arse right back into prison."

Ruben scowled. "There's one demon who won't mind. I just need to find him."

"Good luck with that."

Stung by Isaac's attitude, Ruben snapped, "I'll find him. His scent is unique. Sexy. Warm. Like..."

Isaac interrupted with a splintering crack of laughter. "He smells?"

"No more than you." Ruben sighed, pushing aside the thought of Victor. "I'm a 'nose'—you know, like guys who blend perfume? Except I blend coffee. Well, I used to. My father told me it wasn't a suitable occupation for an angel."

"Daddy's always right," Raul said softly.

Now it was Ruben's turn to snort. "Yeah. So he says."

Raul gave him an unreadable look. "He sent us to get you out of trouble. Be a little grateful."

"To you, yes. To him... I'm not so sure."

Ruben lapsed into silence as they drove along wide streets. Ice and snow grazed the pavements and had turned to slush in the road. People and demons went about their business. Ruben paid special attention to the passing demons, looking first for their horns and then for the bulge of their tails. A couple of free-spirited demon girls in short skirts actually waggled their tails when they saw him staring from the car window, and Ruben grinned in appreciation.

Isaac nodded ahead. "The cathedral. We will drop you there."

"Okay." Ruben set his makeshift bag on his lap and waited as the Mercedes drove over a bridge and into what looked like the older part of the city. The cathedral square had a few students in long scarves milling around but was otherwise empty, and no one paid any attention when Isaac parked the car and turned off the engine.

Ruben gazed up at the front of the cathedral, admiring its clean, solid lines and straightforward construction. The bells sounded the hour—midday—and when the tolls faded into silence, Raul turned to face him again.

He felt in his coat pocket and drew out a crumpled spell-cast. Handing it over, he said, "This is a dual-use spell-cast for use within the DTM, and the DTM only. Don't try casting yourself back to Brazil, because it won't work. You get two trips on this, so use it wisely."

"Thanks." Ruben examined the spell-cast then tucked it inside his coat alongside the rolled wad of five hundred euro.

Raul unfastened his seatbelt. "If you want to try that spell for your wings, you might want to look for a convergence of ley lines, or at least a site of strong energy that sits on a ley line. The more power you can add to the spell, the more successful you'll be—guaranteed."

"Stonehenge?" Ruben wondered aloud.

"That's so cliché." Raul got out of the Mercedes and opened the door for him. "And it's too obvious. Educate yourself. Choose somewhere unlikely. In a short time, the obvious places will have cops swarming all over waiting to pick you up."

Ruben took a tight grip on his few belongings and

climbed out of the car. "Where are you going?"

"Back to Switzerland. We've done our job."

"Do you regret it?" The question hung in the air between them, and Ruben felt the need to clarify. "Losing your wings, I mean."

Raul wore a haunted look, and it took him a moment to respond. "Yes." His gaze wavered as Isaac got out of the driver's seat and leaned his arms on the roof of the car. "But I have Isaac. He gave up everything for me, too."

"And are you happy as a human?" Ruben asked quietly.

He received another cryptic look. "Happiness is all relative."

"Great. A straight answer."

Raul shrugged. "I love Isaac. He loves me. We are fortunate. Things could have been different, but it wasn't meant to be."

There was something else going on here. Ruben frowned. "What do you mean?"

Raul and Isaac shared a look, then Raul said, "Your father had very definite ideas about how my role in the Swiss operation was to end."

"My father?" Ruben echoed, his frown deepening.

Surprise lit Raul's face. "He organized and ran the whole mission. I thought... You didn't know?"

"Why should he know?" Isaac muttered. "Daddy doesn't trust him."

"Isaac." Raul shot him a warning glance.

Isaac ignored his lover and spoke directly to Ruben. "Your father planned the operation for Raul to seduce me. He intended to have Raul killed at the end of it. I couldn't let that happen, so we chose to become human."

"Why?" Ruben blurted.

"Because I love him." Isaac's face was implacable, without any trace of emotion.

Raul ducked his head, blushing.

Ruben stared at them both. That wasn't what he'd meant, but it didn't matter. His mind whirled with this new information, his heartbeat thumping as he considered his next move. "My father is sometimes a bastard, but..."

"He is evil," Isaac said simply. "Why else would he cut off his own son's wings?"

"Isaac!" Raul almost shouted, but it was too late.

Ruben clung to the top of the car as the world

seemed to spin around him. He took a deep breath to clear his head of the sudden dizziness, but nothing could take away the heavy feeling of dread that thudded into the pit of his stomach. "What?"

"You heard." Isaac looked at him over the roof of the Mercedes. "Your wings. That was your father's doing. He cut them from you himself and spell-cast you into the DTM as a diversion."

Raul put his hands to his head. "Isaac, please. He didn't need to know that."

"He's stupid and annoying but he deserves the truth." Isaac's icy gaze silenced his lover before he returned his attention to Ruben.

"A diversion?" Ruben tried not to shiver at the cold, almost demonic look in Isaac's eyes. He wondered what the diversion could be—was it something to do with the plane crash and with Valentin? Uncertainty lodged a lump in his throat, and he swallowed it, trying to regain his bravado. He stared at Isaac. "I don't believe you."

Isaac shrugged. "I don't care if you believe me or not. It's the truth. He used you, just like he used me and Raul. Your father doesn't care about anything but himself." He fixed Ruben with a hard look. "Take my advice—go somewhere far away from him and start a new life. If you try to go back home, he'll destroy you."

CHAPTER 9

Victor scuffed through the drifted snow in the wooded parkland near Turku cathedral. A group of demon and human children shrieked with laughter a short distance away as they hurled snowballs at each other and ran around the trees. Their parents sat on dusted-off benches nearby, chatting and drinking coffee from cardboard cups. Victor closed his eyes as he caught the scent of the hot, sweet beverage. He'd tried hard not to give in to the temptation of the drug since he'd been relieved of his duties in the safe house, but his mood kept dipping and he longed for something to perk him up.

He fingered Ruben's feather through the thin plastic bag inside his coat pocket. God, how could he have been so stupid? Allowing his emotions to get in the way had resulted in this state of humiliation. Not only had he made a fool of himself in front of his Finnish colleagues, he'd almost got Emil sacked for tampering with the DTM mainframe, and he hadn't been able to get anything useful out of Ruben.

Victor cringed with shame at the memory of his late night meeting with Adolfo Oscar. The Head of Station H had driven up from Helsinki to berate him for his poor results and bad attitude. "You're just like your father," Adolfo had told him, his voice as cold as the look in his eyes. "I expected more of you, Officer Bischoff. I was led to believe you could follow orders. I was told you had a healthy respect for authority. Instead I find you willfully hacking into our computer system!"

He'd tried to explain, but Adolfo had silenced him with a glare. "Officer Olsen will take charge of this case now. You will remain here in Turku until our systems analysts have ascertained exactly how much damage you caused with your illegal intrusion into the mainframe. Only then shall we decide what will be done with you."

The instinct for self-preservation almost pushed him to offer the feather he'd found at Hamënlinna, but he'd decided to keep quiet. Chances were he'd never see Ruben again, and the white and blue-black feather was the only thing he had of the wicked, sexy angel. He'd already committed a crime against his own government, so what was one more infraction?

This morning he'd tried to call his father from his hotel room, but when he heard the clicks on the line as he waited for the connection, Victor knew the phone was bugged. He dropped the call before Valdemar answered. It was bad enough that everyone suspected his father of double-dealing with the FIA. There was no point in adding to Valdemar's burden. No doubt he'd be informed soon enough about his son's transgression.

His shoulders hunched against the cold, Victor trudged up a gravel-strewn icy path to the Vartiovuoren Observatory on top of the hill. He gazed down the slope at the city beneath him, the skyline glinting with frost. Though the sun shone over Turku, heavy snow-clouds hung in the distance.

Victor drew in a breath, feeling the sharpness of the air. He dug his hands further into his pockets as he wondered what he should do. Obey orders, obviously. The only way he'd be able to salvage his position in Oxford would be to get his head down and keep out of trouble. If that meant toeing the company line, he'd do it. After all, it wasn't just for his sake alone.

He sighed. A week ago, this had all been so different. He'd been a good agent, an officer with an exemplary record, noticed by senior DTM staff and earmarked for a glittering future despite the family name—and now... Now he didn't know what he was.

Gloom settled around him and he bowed his head, his hair falling forward into his face. His chest tightened with the suppression of emotion, and he shoved angrily at his wings of hair, pushing them back. He turned, his shoes scraping on the scatter of salted grit on the path. Out of the corner of his eye he caught sight of movement and swung around, his senses alert.

"Victor." Ruben emerged from the shadow of the observatory building. Tousle-haired and with his skin flushed pink with cold, he looked every bit as gorgeous—and dangerous—as he'd been yesterday in the copse of the safe house garden.

Victor retreated a few steps, his heart hammering and lazy desire curling inside him. "What are you doing here?"

Ruben shrugged as he came towards him. "Olsen gave me a day off for good behaviour." He pulled a pass from his pocket and held it up, and Victor saw with relief that it was a DTM-approved permit.

Relaxing slightly, Victor smiled. "Well. It's nice of them to let you out. You'll be able to go shopping. Buy some more clothes, maybe, in colors you actually like rather than grey and black."

"I kinda like grey and black." Ruben indicated his jeans and pulled a section of his jumper out between the buttons of his coat to show that he was wearing the grey sweater Victor had chosen for him.

Victor brushed a strand of hair from his eyes, the gesture nervous rather than necessary. "It suits you."

They stood looking at one another in silence for a while, then Ruben laughed. "Wow, this is awkward."

"Yes. Sorry." Victor's mood fractured and his

shoulders slumped.

"Don't be." Ruben put his hands in his pockets and rocked back on his heels. "I'm sorry I got you fired from your job."

"It wasn't you. I..." Victor hesitated, then decided to tell him. "I couldn't find Valentin Tristan in any of the files, so I hacked the DTM's mainframe. They found out and took me off the case."

Ruben gave him a shrewd look. "Because you hacked the mainframe or because they didn't want you to see Valentin's file?"

Victor stared at him as the idea took root. "I'm not sure. I assumed it was because of the hack, but now you mention it..." His voice tailed off as he considered the ramifications of what Ruben had just said.

"What is it?" Ruben tilted his head, curiosity in his eyes. "You look worried."

Victor bit his lip. He was worried—for himself and for his father. The situation rang alarm bells whichever way he looked at it. He forced a smile. "Just an idle thought. It's nothing. Shall we walk? It's getting cold standing around here."

"Sure. I've got nothing better to do."

Ruben fell into step beside him, positioning himself just slightly too close for Victor's comfort.

The sunlight cast their merged shadows ahead of them on the path, and Victor pulled away, disturbed and turned-on by their proximity. When Ruben shot him a quizzical look, Victor tried to think of an excuse for his behaviour. In a flash of inspiration, he turned and walked backwards, glancing around the park. "Where's your tail?"

Ruben swept him with a hot, lingering gaze. "You're the one with the tail, buttercup."

"Not that kind of tail!" Victor blushed, remembering all too well how good it had felt to have Ruben between his thighs, playing with his tail. His belly tightened with a kick of lust, and he hurried on: "If they've let you out on a day-pass, you'll have one of the demons from the safe house tailing you discreetly."

"Oh." Ruben gave a careless laugh. "They must be very discreet, then. I haven't noticed anyone."

"That's strange. They're usually so obvious." Turning full circle, Victor scanned the area, studying the group of parents with their children before looking at other random people strolling through the park. "Maybe it's that guy there, with the newspaper."

"So what? As long as they don't interfere with my day, there could be fifty demons tailing me for all I care." Ruben sounded grumpy. "Anyway, I'm with you. You're a demon, even if they sacked you. They can't complain."

His response made Victor slightly suspicious. In the week they'd known one another, Ruben had never shown irritation or annoyance—at least not in front of Victor. On many occasions he'd known when Ruben ducked the truth or told an outright blatant lie, mainly because he was so outrageous when he did it, so this irritable dismissal made Victor wonder if Ruben was being evasive now.

The suspicion wasn't fully formed, but Victor decided to follow his instinct. "How did you find me, anyway?"

"Coincidence." Ruben gave him a big, bright smile, but it soon faded, replaced by an anxious look. "No, it wasn't." He paused for a moment, then sighed. "I don't want to lie to you, Victor. I like you too much to lie to you."

Victor felt his heart thump. Trying to keep his tone neutral, he asked, "So you were lying to me before, about Valentin Tristan and the plane crash?"

"No. That was the truth." Ruben halted on the path and faced him. "I found you because I could smell you."

"Smell me?" Shocked and more than a little dismayed by this revelation, Victor tried to sniff surreptitiously under his arms. "What do you mean, you could smell me?"

Ruben laughed. "I'm a nose."

Victor wrinkled his own nose and frowned. "You blend perfume?"

"Oh, you're smart. No. I used to blend coffee." Ruben gave him a sidelong glance, as if judging the impact of his words.

"So you did work for your father." Victor tamped down on his surge of interest, reminding himself to play this cool. This wasn't an official interrogation, after all, but now he had his own reasons for asking.

"Yes and no." Ruben skidded down the rest of the slope to the bottom of the hill and swung on the park gate, holding it open for Victor to pass. "Not all coffee beans are created equal, even the ones grown on the Barbosa plantations. My father punishes the growers of inferior quality beans—" Ruben grimaced, leaving Victor in no doubt that Barbosa Senior was a hard taskmaster, "and he rewards those who present him with the finest, smoothest end product. But coffee is rarely drunk pure from one source. Like heroin, it's blended, good stuff with less good stuff, mediocre stuff with bad stuff... and that's where I came in."

They left the park, picking their way over packed snow frozen solid and wading through ankle-deep slush as they negotiated the pavements. Victor trod warily, his mind spinning as he tried to remember everything Ruben was telling him. If only he could stop somewhere and jot it all down in his DTM notebook. Hell, he'd write it on the back of his hand if he could. This stuff was important.

His focus was so intense he didn't notice a patch of black ice. A second later he slipped. He windmilled his arms and let out an undignified squawk, which turned into a whimper when Ruben grabbed him and tucked an arm around his waist. Bent almost backwards, Victor stared up into Ruben's eyes and got lost in that velvety brown gaze.

Ruben gave him a crooked smile and leaned closer, and Victor came to his senses. He leapt upright, skidded on the ice again, then clung to a lamppost. Recalling himself to their conversation, Victor demanded, "So you were responsible for the coffee blends?"

"Not just responsible, I invented half of them," Ruben said with a touch of arrogance. He lifted his chin and held himself straight with pride before he snorted and went back to slouching. He tapped his nose. "My father would tell me what grade of coffee he wanted to produce, and I'd create it. I knew how to make a blend that tasted good when in reality it was made from an inferior crop."

Victor let go of the lamppost. "Your father must have been proud of your ability."

Ruben scowled. "You would think."

"He wasn't?" The ice seemed less slippery around the lamppost. Victor went a few steps and turned back for Ruben, who followed, his hands in his pockets and a black look on his face.

"Being a nose is considered low-class. Making one's living with one's hands—or nose—is for poor people, not for rich angels. Certainly not for angels of the Barbosa family." Bitterness oozed from every word, and Ruben's eyes flashed with suppressed emotion. He walked faster, heedless of the icy pavements. "I loved being a nose. I loved blending coffee. But one day my father told me to stop. I was too old to play silly games any more, he said. It was time I remembered who I was. As if I could forget!"

He looked magnificent in his anger, and Victor felt a complicated tug between pity and awe. "How old were you when he said that?"

"I'd just turned eighteen. I was angry. I still am." Ruben gave him a brilliant, vicious smile. "That's when I came into my inheritance. I bought my first yacht and started sleeping with as many pretty blond boys as I could get my hands on—and believe me, I got my hands on a lot."

Jealousy knifed into Victor's heart, a shaft of splintered cold so painful it made him turn his head sharply so Ruben wouldn't see his reaction. Victor looked into a shop window as they walked passed, staring so hard his vision blurred. "You were determined to punish your father with your lifestyle."

Ruben snorted. "You make it sound so stuffy, buttercup."

Victor had no intention of pursuing that line of

conversation. He didn't want to hear about the long line of lovers Ruben had enjoyed. He paused in front of another shop window and realised he was looking at a display of perfumes. When Ruben came to stand beside him, Victor asked, "You could really smell me?"

"Yes." Ruben gave him another searching look.

Nervous, shy, Victor ducked his head. "Do I still smell of honeysuckle and sea grass?"

Ruben smiled and moved closer, lifting a hand to brush back Victor's hair. "And olive oil on old gold, and the first frost of autumn... Yes, you do. I've smelled thousands of fragrances, but yours is the most unique, the most perfect scent I've ever found. The notes of your skin, your hair... you're a delight to my senses."

Victor thought his legs had turned to jelly. "That's how you found me in the park. You traced me by my scent."

"Like a bloodhound." Ruben leaned closer and whispered a kiss over Victor's lips.

It was light, teasing, a promise—and then Victor pulled back, blushing fiercely as an elderly woman with a trolley barged past, tutting and muttering at their behaviour.

They looked at each other and grinned, then resumed walking. Victor pressed his cold hands to the warmth of the blush in his cheeks, while Ruben looked pleased with himself. "There's nothing wrong with public displays of affection," he said. "No wonder this country is so cold and grey! People should be more open with one another. Hug more. Laugh more. Dance more." He made a few samba moves, skidding through the slush in the road.

Victor shook his head. It would be so easy to allow himself to become infected by Ruben's irrepressible spirit, but where would that leave him? By the end of the day, the not-very-efficient DTM tail would appear to take Ruben back to the safe house, and nothing would have changed. Ruben would still be a prisoner, and Victor would still be in disgrace.

With a heavy sigh, Victor resumed his questioning. To Hell with being subtle. If he only had a limited time with Ruben, he couldn't afford to waste a single moment. Catching hold of Ruben's arm as he attempted a crisscross botafogo, Victor blurted out, "What do you know about the black market smuggling rings into the DTM?"

Ruben stopped dancing. "So this is an interrogation, is it?"

Victor blushed. "I'm not wearing a wire, if that's what you mean."

"Don't be so po-faced, buttercup. I know you're not. I'd have been able to smell it." He grinned and cha-cha-cha'd backwards into the road, bumped into the boot of a parked BMW, and set off the car alarm.

Victor winced away from the shriek of the alarm. "You can smell hidden microphones?"

Ruben covered his ears and laughed as he retreated a short distance down the street away from the car. Victor chased after him, feeling ridiculous. The angel would be the death of him, he was sure of it. As they turned a corner and reached the path that ran alongside the river, Victor said, "Elias, please. I need to know what you know about the smuggling."

Ruben shot him a pointed look. "Why?"

"It's personal."

Ruben stood motionless, staring at him.

Victor wavered. Could he trust Ruben? Hell, yes— he'd rather trust Ruben than anybody else, including, at the moment, his own father. With this in mind, Victor said, "I think—I'm afraid..." He hesitated then pushed the words out, avoiding Ruben's curious look: "I think my father may be involved with the smuggling rings."

Ruben's gaze sharpened. "Your father?"

The path was empty, but still Victor looked both ways before he tucked his arm through Ruben's and drew him into the shelter of a stone-built pavilion. Lowering his voice, Victor murmured, "There's something going on here, something I can't explain. A week ago, I was shown pictures of you with your wings and your lovers on a yacht—pictures my father took. He's been living under suspicion for years, but he's never told me what for... but I think I've found out."

Ruben leaned against the wall, his expression shuttered. "What?"

"When I was searching for the file on Valentin Tristan, when I hacked the DTM mainframe, I found something." Victor took a deep breath to calm his trembling nerves. "Valentin used to work for us. For the DTM. He defected five years ago to the FIA. There's the suggestion that my father was involved."

Ruben frowned. "Wait. I thought you said your father was involved with the coffee smuggling?"

Victor withdrew his hand from where it still rested in the crook of Ruben's arm. He needed to get his head straight, and even the most innocent touch made his concentration wobble. "I think the two things are connected. I think... I think my father brokered the deal with the FIA to return Monaco to the DTM in exchange for running the coffee smuggling operation. I think my dad's a double agent."

His words met a blank look and a long silence. Just as Victor began to wonder if Ruben had actually heard what he'd said, the angel shifted slightly. "Are you sure?"

"Of course not! That's why I needed your help.

Why I need your help." Victor gave him a desperate look. "I don't want to believe it. I don't want it to be true, but I need to know, Elias. I need to find out. If I can clear his name..."

"I'll help you." Ruben pushed away from the wall and stood straight.

Gratitude filled Victor in a rush, making him babble. "I can give you the feather. I have it with me. Look." He started to fumble in his pocket for the evidence bag.

"Forget about the feather for now." Ruben fixed him with his gaze. "First of all, who is your father?"

"Valdemar Bischoff. The Monaco Resident. He's been the Monaco Resident for twenty years, which is unusual. He should be a Controller by now, but they kept him there—even when Monaco was ruled by the FIA. And then..."

"Shh." Ruben placed a finger over Victor's lips. "The coffee—or at least the coffee from Brazil, which is shipped out by Barbosa Enterprises via Colombia—is smuggled into DTM territory through Schönefeld airport in Berlin. I thought everyone knew that."

Victor frowned in confusion. "Everyone? Why?"

A small smile tugged at Ruben's lips. "The Berlin Resident has a... fondness, shall we say, for the angel who runs the smuggling ring."

"The Berlin Resident is Ludwig Wiedemann." It took a few seconds for Victor to realise what Ruben meant. "Oh! You mean Ludwig and—and—"

"Mario-Ramon Diez," Ruben supplied with a grin. "Yes. Exactly. So the Berlin Resident turns his back and looks the other way when a coffee shipment comes in. I honestly don't know what happens to it after it's landed at Schönefeld, but I do know that once it leaves Berlin, the smugglers are fair game for German DTM officers. Ludwig Wiedemann only protects Diez and his lieutenants; he doesn't extend the same courtesy to anyone else."

"God, what a mess." Victor leaned back against the dressed stone of the pavilion and shivered. He glanced out at the street and realised it was snowing. Thick, soft flakes whirled past, the flurries thickening as he watched. He tried to untangle the thoughts crowding his head, but felt even more lost than before. He rubbed his temples. "I need to write all this down to try and make sense of it."

"If it helps, I don't think your father is involved in the smuggling." Ruben's voice sounded soft and sympathetic.

Victor nodded. "Thank you. I'm grateful."

"I don't want your gratitude." Ruben took a step closer, intent in his eyes.

His heart stuttered and his stomach swooped low,

leaving Victor feeling hollow and needy. He squashed against the wall, trying to ignore his rising desire. "The feather," he whispered. "You'll want the feather."

"No." Ruben put a hand on the wall beside Victor's head, penning him in. "I want you to be honest with me."

A nervous laugh crackled out of him. "I've been honest!"

"You haven't." Lifting his hand, Ruben stroked Victor's face.

Victor let out his breath in a whoosh. Ruben's touch was warm and gentle, and it was all he could do to stop himself from fitting the curve of his cheek to the palm of Ruben's hand. A moment later, Ruben took his hand away, and Victor felt oddly bereft. He covered his confusion by asking, "What do you mean?"

Before Ruben could reply, a young woman walked past with a dog. The animal pulled on its leash and barked at them, and the mood shattered. Victor and Ruben drew apart as the young woman scolded the dog for its behaviour and pulled it away down the riverside path.

Ruben smiled, apparently glad of the distraction. "Anyway, I thought you were trying to interrogate me, not letting me into your darkest secrets."

Embarrassment twisted his gut, and Victor edged

away from the pavilion with another anxious laugh. "I haven't mentioned any of my darkest secrets."

"Maybe you should." Ruben grinned, his earlier expression now replaced by his usual cheeky, confident look. "Forget the boring stuff and skip straight to the ones involving me."

This time, Victor's laughter was genuine. "I don't think so."

Ruben leaned close and kissed him. "Let's get out of the cold."

* * *

Warmth and the comforting smell of coffee hung around them as they sat at a table in a little cafe. Ruben glanced around at the clientele. Many were blond, some were pretty, but none were as spectacular as Victor, who sat opposite him with his hands around a large mug of macchiato and an expression of pure bliss on his face.

Ruben propped his chin on his hands and watched him sip the drink. Each taste made Victor quiver, and Ruben thought he understood now why the demons were so hung up on coffee. He knew it was some kind of drug for them, but he'd never been sure how much of that was FIA propaganda. Angels were immune to any kind of caffeine side-effect, and while Ruben enjoyed coffee more than many angels, in the end it was just a drink.

For Victor, it seemed to be like liquid sex.

The thought amused him, and Ruben hid his grin. He couldn't be jealous of a cup of coffee, no matter how orgasmic Victor looked as he raised the drink to his lips again.

"So," Ruben began, and Victor shot him a pleading look over the top of his cup.

"Wait. Please. Just wait until I finish this?"

Ruben nodded. "Okay." He drained his frappucino and leaned back in the chair. While Victor was engaged in holy communion with his macchiato, Ruben considered their earlier conversations. He'd never heard of the Monaco Resident Valdemar Bischoff and couldn't care less whether or not Valdemar was a double agent, but if it mattered to Victor, then Ruben decided it would matter to him, too.

He toyed with his empty cup. Damn, but he shouldn't get so involved in shit. His father often accused him of not making plans and just drifting through life, and this was a pretty good example of him screwing up because of lack of foresight. His interest in Victor had started out as lust, plain and simple, but now it was getting complicated—and not just because Victor had managed to resist him for a week.

Victor occupied his thoughts almost eighty percent of the time. That was serious. Even worse, most of those thoughts weren't even pornographic. Ruben had a whole series of sweet, fluffy thoughts about Victor alongside the achingly hot X-rated thoughts, which were tucked up against the deep, serious thoughts and—most scary of all—the nebulous idea that Victor could be It. The One. His Soul Mate and True Love.

Ruben crushed the plastic frappucino cup in his hand. Angels didn't fall in love with demons. They were enemies, or at least they weren't supposed to like one another very much. No, he should just have fun with Victor, fuck him silly and then say goodbye. There'd be other pretty blonds to seduce in the future.

Anguish clutched at his heart. Ruben felt irritated. Shit, he was turning all emo over a cute little demon. He needed to toughen up and forget all the gestures of kindness and the friendly smiles and the horny horns and the kinky tail and the sexy body. Victor was just a demon.

Ruben glared across the table at him, and melted a little when Victor put down his coffee cup and licked foam from his upper lip. Ruben's brain short-circuited and his cock twitched. He had to get himself under control.

Taking a deep breath, Ruben sat forward again and took the cup. "Another?"

Victor gave him a slightly spaced-out look. "Sure."

"Maybe not. You look drunk." Ruben moved the

cup away.

"I'm not!" Victor wagged a finger at him. "I am completely sober. Caffeine takes time to affect a demon. In half an hour I'll feel it, but not now."

"With British coffee, maybe. This is Finnish coffee," Ruben reminded him, amused. "It's full-strength. It'll hit you straight away."

"Oh." Victor gazed at him, looking adorably befuddled. "I should have a drink of water, then."

An idea unfurled in his mind, and Ruben got to his feet. "No. I'll bring you another coffee. Stay there."

"You want to get me high?" Victor asked, trying to look disapproving.

"Buttercup, you're already high," Ruben said over his shoulder as he headed for the counter. He stood in line and asked for a refill of the macchiato, paid for it from the stash of euro Officer Olsen had given him, and then took the drink over the extras shelf. He hesitated over whether Victor would prefer chocolate sprinkles or a shake of cinnamon powder, and while he thought about it, he took the bottle of sleeping pills from his coat pocket and tapped five into the coffee before he could change his mind.

He plucked a wooden stirrer from a tray and swirled it through the macchiato, probing with the end of the spill until he could no longer detect the shape of the pills. Then he added cinnamon and chocolate sprinkles before carrying the cup back to Victor.

"Oh, you're so wicked." Victor gave him a lazy, seductive look as he accepted the coffee.

Ruben sat, tension gnawing at him as he watched Victor drink. He worried that Victor would taste the bitterness of the sleeping pills, but after one macchiato he was already three sheets to the wind and didn't seem capable of noticing anything beyond the heavenly hit of caffeine.

What he was doing was unfair, not to mention illegal. Ruben knew that, but he also knew Victor represented his only hope of regenerating his wings. Victor deserved better than to be rendered senseless by a large dose of sleeping tablets and abducted from Turku, but it was the only way Ruben's plan—half-baked though it was—would come to fruition. He needed a demon, and he needed a ley line. Victor had already broken DTM rules, and Ruben wasn't about to ask him to break even more. No, this was the best way forward. Drug Victor, use the dual spell-casts Raul had given him to get out of Finland, find a ley line, and shag Victor until the spell took effect and Ruben's wings grew back.

As a bonus, he knew Victor had one of his feathers. Ruben had no idea if that would help in the regeneration process, but maybe it would get things going. It wouldn't hurt to try.

He began to relax as Victor gulped down the

coffee. It seemed as if he truly didn't notice anything different about the drink. By the time he'd drained the macchiato to the dregs, the gritty residue of the pills had melted away and Ruben knew he was in the clear. He kept a careful watch on Victor, noting the heaviness of his eyelids and the way he kept slurring or forgetting his words, and then the listless, sleepy movements he made.

"Elias. Tired." Victor slumped forward over the table, trying to support his head in his hands. His elbows skidded in opposite directions and he almost fell face-first into his empty cup.

Ruben caught him. "I think you've had enough," he said loudly, for the benefit of the other demons and humans sitting nearby. A couple of people laughed sympathetically and returned to their own conversations as Ruben stood and pulled Victor to his feet.

"Oopsie." Victor stumbled against him and buried his face in Ruben's neck. "Mm. You smell good."

"Time to go home!" Ruben declared, hooking an arm around Victor's waist and supporting him as he almost lurched into another table. Pulling Victor back against his side, Ruben guided him out of the cafe and onto the street.

Victor giggled and hummed a little tune as they wobbled along. Evening was falling, and darkness wrapped around them. Ruben headed for the cathedral, half holding, half dragging Victor along with him. People hurried past, and no one paid them any attention. Ruben supposed caffeine-high demons must be a common sight in Turku.

"Angel, angel," Victor sang before he dissolved into laughter.

Ruben tried to hush him, glancing around. A man up ahead of them on the street turned back to look, then lingered for a while. Cursing under his breath, Ruben ushered Victor to the other side of the road and shunted him towards the cathedral square. After a minute, Ruben checked over his shoulder and saw the man standing beneath a lamp on the far side of the square. The light glinted on two little horns, and Ruben felt anxiety twist his belly.

Every other demon he'd encountered today had ignored him. This one seemed suspicious. Ruben nudged Victor closer to the cathedral steps, slinging an arm around his shoulders to make him hurry. Glancing back again, he saw the other demon move forwards as if he intended on accosting them.

Before he could decide what to do for the best, Victor swayed against Ruben's chest. "They told me not to trust you. Devious angel." He tripped over his own feet and giggled, pressing closer to Ruben. "Told me not to fall in love with you. Fuck you, yes, but not love you..."

Startled, Ruben stared at him. "You haven't fucked me yet, and you certainly don't love me."

Victor attempted to drape his arms around Ruben's neck and gazed up at him, his eyes huge and soft. "I do. I do. Or I think I do. It's so confusing."

"You're doped up on caffeine," Ruben said baldly. "You'd declare your love to a lamppost."

"I love you, Ruben Patrick Barbosa." Victor made a grand dramatic gesture, flinging his arm out, and almost fell over.

"Okay, you love me. That's great." Guilt spiked him, and Ruben wished he hadn't used quite so many sleeping pills.

He checked over his shoulder again and realised the other demon had vanished. While it could have been a good sign, Ruben felt his wing stumps itch with unease. He pulled the spell-cast from his pocket and examined the instructions. Spell-casts only took effect within designated zones, usually hubs such as railway stations, airports, cathedrals or other places of worship, university campuses, and other such places—but before he activated the spell-cast, he had to ask Victor where the best ley lines were located.

Victor grabbed him, clinging to the front of Ruben's coat as he tried to look serious and alluring at the same time. "Let's have sex."

Ruben smiled. "Tempting. Very tempting. But not here and not now."

"Please." Victor hiccupped and slumped against

him again. "Elias... you were right. I am a virgin. Sort of. Kind of. Maybe. Do blowjobs count? Not the one you did to me yesterday. That was the most amazing blowjob of my life. I haven't done anything else apart from blowjobs. Does that make me a virgin?"

"Hush, buttercup. Not so loud."

Victor swung on his arm. "Does it, Elias? Does it?"

"Technically, yes, but—" Ruben stopped, his senses on high alert as his wing stumps fluffed with a premonition of danger. He took a sharp breath as, seconds later, he heard the wail of sirens in the distance.

The demons were coming for him, and if they caught him here with Victor, they'd both be punished. This was it. Time to cast the spell.

He maneuvered Victor onto the cathedral steps and wrapped his arms around him. He'd never done a dual-person spell-cast before and he hoped they both ended up in the same place. Then there was the problem of knowing where the Hell to go. Desperately he poked Victor in the side to get his attention. "Is Radcliffe Camera on a ley line?"

Victor looked at him, his focus slightly fuzzy. "Radcliffe Camera? No. I'll tell you what is, though. Stonehenge. Glastonbury. Avebury. West Kennet Long Barrow. Silbury Hill. Woodhenge."

Ruben propped him up as Victor started to topple over. "Anywhere else?"

"Rosslyn Chapel. The Lizard. The Rollrights. Castlerigg." Victor's head drooped onto Ruben's chest. "Can't remember the rest, sorry."

"It's okay." Ruben pressed a kiss to Victor's head. He had plenty of options to choose from now. He just hoped it worked.

Victor stirred against him, snuggling closer. "Take me to bed."

"Tomorrow," Ruben promised, shuffling them into position and holding up the spell-cast to activate it. "We'll do it tomorrow, okay?"

"I love you, Elias. I really do." Victor kissed him just as the spell took hold. Energy sparked through them, joining them for an instant in a blaze of power before they were swallowed up by the night.

CHAPTER 10

Victor groaned. His eyelids seemed glued shut and his brain was doing a samba around his skull. He tried to lift his head from the pillow but the effort was too much. Flopping back down, he realised two things simultaneously: he was lying on something hard and cold and most definitely not a bed, and he was completely naked.

Startled, Victor opened his eyes. Daylight swam across his vision, a stark brightness that stabbed like knives. Nausea climbed his throat, and he turned his face to the side, gasping with effort. His cheek brushed damp, chilly stone. Slowly, he opened his eyes a little at a time, veiling his sight with his lashes until his head stopped aching and the urge to throw up had retreated.

He tried to move and realised it wasn't the caffeine hangover that was responsible for his lack of mobility. He was tied down, wrists bound with hemp rope above his head. When he jerked his hands, he felt the slight burn of the rope against his skin. Gritting his teeth, he pulled hard, ignoring the discomfort, and heard the creak of something wooden behind him. Tilting his head, Victor saw that the ropes were tied around a pew.

He was in a church.

Victor blinked and shook the disordered fall of hair from his eyes as he looked around. He winced at the sunlight through the clear quarries in the stained glass windows, then drew in his breath at the riot of stonework around him. Demons, angels, skeletons, and green men danced and leered at him from every surface. Dramatic foliage hewn from the stone blocks hung above him. Strange symbols surrounded him. In places, the walls and ceiling were flocked with colorful lichen. A heavy sense of stillness lay over the church, giving Victor the sense that this almost wasn't a church but something else, something greater.

He wriggled again, trying to work his ankles free of the rope that held them fastened to an elaborately decorated pillar. Some more twisting and turning, and Victor realised the bench he was tied to was, in fact, an altar.

He lay still, his mind whirling, trying to concentrate through the fog of caffeine-induced muddle. What the Hell had happened last night? He remembered meeting Ruben in the park and going to the cafe with him. He remembered drinking two— was it only two?—macchiatos before he felt uncharacteristically out of control. Ruben had reminded him this was Finnish coffee, stronger than the watery decaffeinated brews he was accustomed to in England. True, but still... he shouldn't have been this susceptible.

Victor groaned. It hurt to think, and he hadn't managed to figure out how he'd got from a cafe in Turku—no, wait, they'd gone outside—the cathedral in Turku, then, to this place. Wherever this place was. He didn't think he was in Finland any more. Had Ruben kidnapped him? The thought seemed unbelievable. Ruben had no need to kidnap him. Victor blushed at the memory of how he'd offered himself to Ruben on the steps of the cathedral, and Ruben had turned him down. Hell, how embarrassing!

Though not as embarrassing as being tied naked to an altar in a really odd-looking church. Victor gave another tug at his bonds and glanced around again, wondering why Ruben had chosen to tie him up here. Perhaps the angel had a kinky fantasy about making love in a church. If so, Victor wished Ruben had simply asked him about it first. Of course, he would have refused—which was probably why Ruben had kidnapped him and tied him up.

A deep sigh escaped Victor's lips. He wriggled the pointed end of his tail from beneath his thigh and let the tip flick back and forth as he thought. The chilly air danced over his skin, tightening his nipples and raising goose-bumps over his body. Humiliating though it would be, he hoped someone would turn up soon and free him before he got too cold and froze to death.

Just as that thought crossed his mind, the side door in the north wall of the church banged open. Victor strained to see who'd entered, but a pillar blocked his line of sight. He heard the click of a lock and then silence descended once more. A moment later, jaunty footsteps sounded across the stone-flagged floor and Ruben appeared.

"Hey, you're awake." Ruben hurried over to him, his eyes sparkling and his cheeks flushed with cold. A dusting of snowflakes melted in his hair and on his shoulders. He shrugged out of his coat and slung it over the stone railing separating the altar from the nave. "I didn't mean to leave you alone when you were tied up, but I was hungry and I wasn't sure how long it would take for the sleeping tablets to wear off, and—"

Sleeping tablets? Victor stared at him. "Ruben! What's going on? What have you done? Where—"

Ruben placed a finger over Victor's lips. "All in good time, buttercup. God, you look amazing naked." He blushed slightly then continued, "I knew you would. I couldn't help myself. Sorry if you're cold, but things should heat up in a moment."

"Heat up? What are you talking about?" Victor felt his eyes widen as Ruben pulled off his sweater and started unbuttoning his shirt. By the time the garment was half undone, exposing the sexy smudge of dark hair on Ruben's chest, Victor realised he was staring like a love-struck schoolboy and forced his gaze away. He stared at the ornate ceiling instead. "This isn't some kind of kinky angel fantasy about having sex with a demon in a church, is it?"

"Baby, my fantasies are far kinkier than that." Ruben sounded offended. "But rope-play is an interest of mine, and I really didn't want you to turn over in your sleep and roll off the altar. Better that I tied you down so you wouldn't hurt yourself. Of course, the bonus is that you look really hot in bondage..."

Unable to believe what he was hearing, Victor stared at him again. Big mistake. Ruben's shirt fluttered to the floor as he began unfastening his jeans. Soon Ruben stepped out of them and kicked the jeans aside. Yet again he'd gone without underwear. Yet again it seemed he only needed to glance at Victor to get hard. Yet again Victor felt utterly powerless when he looked at Ruben. It was so unfair. No one, angel, demon or human, had the right to look so sinfully gorgeous.

"Um." Victor felt a wave of prickling, flustered heat spread throughout his body as he stared at Ruben. "Uh, you look pretty good naked, too."

"Better than in the paparazzi shots of me on my yacht?" Ruben preened a little.

"Hell, yes." Victor's mouth had gone dry and the words emerged as a squeak. He cleared his throat and turned his head away, the blush flaming in his face. His cock stirred and began to thicken against his thigh. He couldn't get a hard-on in a church! Frantic, he tried to think of boring things: the thirty-seven times table, a complete chronological list of the founding demons of the DTM, the uses of the ablative absolute...

It wasn't working. All he could focus on was Ruben's naked body, the smooth tawny skin, the hair on his chest and striping down to his groin, his muscles and the curve of his arse, the rampant length of his cock, the tufty, downy-feathered wing stumps and the wicked look in his eyes.

Victor groaned. "I am so in trouble. This is bad."

"No, buttercup." Ruben bent over to rummage through his coat pockets, causing Victor to whimper and his cock to spring to rigid attention. When Ruben straightened, he held the black and white feather between his fingers and smiled. "I'm going to make this so good."

Confusion filtered into Victor's lust-addled mind. "The feather—I mean, your feather..."

Ruben slid the blade of the feather over Victor's lips. "You promised I could have it if I answered your questions."

"I did. And you did. Answer my questions, I mean." Victor shook his head, cursing his slow responses. "You can have it. I only took it as a souvenir."

"A souvenir?" Ruben tickled the tip of the feather over Victor's bound arm, sliding it down over his chest. "I'm flattered you wanted a souvenir of me."

Victor squirmed. "Stop that. It tickles."

"You don't want to laugh when you fuck?" Ruben gave him a puzzled look.

"I told you. I—I haven't... not really..."

Ruben dropped the feather in the middle of Victor's chest and hauled himself up onto the altar, straddling Victor's waist. "I remember. And—" Ruben pulled a regretful face, "I'm sorry our first time together is going to be so ritualistic. It's not what I had planned, but if this is the only way..."

An awareness of something being not quite right crept into Victor's consciousness. His pulse quickened and he strained at the ropes that held him in place. "The only way? What's going on, Elias?"

"I love it when you look flustered." Ruben leaned down and kissed him, his lips sweet and slightly redolent of coffee and maple syrup.

Determined not to respond to the distraction, Victor pulled away, his breathing sharp and his heart fluttering. He tugged at the restraints again. "Elias. Tell me what the Hell you're trying to do here. If this isn't some kinky sex game, then what is it?"

Ruben pouted. "I thought you knew everything." He sat up and edged backwards until Victor's erection nudged between the cheeks of Ruben's arse. He wriggled, rubbing his arse against Victor's cock as his own prick strained higher against his belly. "Damn, you feel good. I'm an equal opportunities angel, buttercup, and while I badly want to spend hours playing with your tail before I sink into your sexy body and ride you hard, for the spell to work I think I have to let you do the fucking."

The sight of that hard, throbbing cock almost made Victor forget what Ruben was saying. Dazed by want, the words finally registered, then the meaning crept into his brain, until Victor finally realised the importance of what Ruben had said.

Victor jerked up from the altar so fast that Ruben had to grab on tight to keep from falling off. "Spell?" Victor gabbled. "I'm here because of a spell?"

Ruben smiled and stroked his hair. "Sure. What did you think—that we were here to take tea with the vicar?"

"Spell!" Victor said again, his mind running through all the possible permutations of angel-and-demon sex magic. Oh God, why hadn't he paid attention in his Practical Magick class? He'd only audited the course, thinking it wouldn't be important in his chosen career. Now he cursed himself for his stupidity. "Spell..."

Ruben crouched low once more, backing up until Victor's cock fit snugly against him. He toyed with the feather he'd laid on Victor's chest. "The spell that will give me back my wings," he said conversationally, as if this was the most normal thing in the world. "The spell that needs to be performed on a ley line. You told me Rosslyn Chapel was on a ley line, so I came here. Now we fuck, and when you orgasm, I'll take your power and my wings will regenerate. And we get to have hot sex at the same time!" Ruben grinned. "Isn't that just awesome?"

The memories of the Practical Magick class returned in a rush and Victor gasped, panic seizing him with a cold grip. Several words came to mind, but 'awesome' wasn't one of them. He moistened his lips with the tip of his tongue. "Elias, while it might be good for you, it won't be good for me."

"Don't be silly, buttercup." Ruben bounced on top of him, then leaned over to root through his coat pockets again, retrieving a small vial of oil. He held it up, its contents glimmering in the light. "I'm going to oil your cock up nice and slow, get you really horny. I could oil your tail, too, if you like. Then I'll..."

"Ruben." A wave of despair crashed over Victor. He shook his head. "Elias, please listen. You can do whatever you like with me—"

Ruben purred. "I hope so."

Victor closed his eyes for a moment. "Elias! You can do whatever you like, but not here! This spell, this regeneration spell... it'll kill me."

A tiny silence dropped between them. Ruben's brow furrowed, then he laughed. "Hey, I know I'm good, but even I don't think I'm that good."

"It's not funny. I'm not making a joke." Victor pulled at the ropes binding his wrists. "Have sex with me, but not here. Not on a ley line. Not with the invocation of magic. It will kill me, Elias. I will die."

Ruben's laughter faded. He shifted on top of Victor, uncertainty clouding his features. "You'll die? For real?"

"Of course for real!" Victor struggled against his bonds again and then gave up with an angry huff. He recited: "Practical Magick 101: A demon's energy may be drained from him or her through sexual intercourse on a ley line. Said energy may be used by the practitioner for their own purposes, either to enhance specific powers or to repair or restore body parts injured or dismembered. Demons of second rank or higher may survive such a drain to their life force, but demons of third rank and below will perish during the energy exchange."

Another silence followed, and then Ruben asked, "What rank do you hold?"

"Third." Victor felt weary. "I'm a third rank demon."

"Oh."

A much longer silence.

"Victor..." Ruben's expression was anguished. "I really want my wings back."

"Can't you go home and have them regenerated there?" Victor gazed up at him, torn between sympathy for the angel's plight and fear for his own safety. "Your father—he's powerful. Can't he spell-cast you a new pair of wings?"

Ruben's expression darkened and his hands clenched so tight that the vial of oil cracked. "Fuck." Ruben flung the vial aside and it smashed on the floor, the sound of breaking glass delicate and musical. He scowled after it, then said through gritted teeth, "I'm not going back. I'm not asking him."

Victor lifted his chin, swallowing his panic. "So you'll kill me instead?"

"No!" Ruben stared at him for a moment, horror in his eyes, then he clambered off Victor and jumped from the altar. He paced across the floor, still naked, then leaned both hands against the wall as if drawing strength from it. His head bowed, he muttered, "Shit. What a mess. What a fucking mess."

"Elias." Wriggling onto his side against the pull of the restraints, Victor managed to face him. "Elias, let me go. I can help you."

Ruben spun around, took two steps back towards

the altar, then stopped. He grabbed his jeans and pulled them on, his movements stiff and staccato. "The only way you can help me is to give me back my wings, but I don't want to kill you!"

"Please."

They stared at one another. A heartbeat passed, then Ruben came over to him, framed Victor's face with his hands, and kissed him. There was no teasing quality to the kiss this time, just raw passion and misery and need. It lasted a long time, and Victor responded to it with everything he had. He felt tears track down Ruben's face, warm and salty where they touched his lips, and then Ruben broke free and whirled away.

Shaken, Victor whispered, "Elias..."

Ruben kept his back turned. "My father cut my wings off."

Horror blossomed in Victor's chest even as he started to make political connections and draw conclusions in his mind. His gaze went to the two downy wing stumps beneath Ruben's shoulder blades, and he saw the tension held in Ruben's back, in the tightness of the muscles. "Oh," he murmured, sorrow coiling in his throat. "Oh, Elias."

"He did it himself." Ruben's voice hitched, but he kept on talking. "Cut off my wings and let me fall, then sent me to Finland."

"Why?" Victor asked, aware that being tied up naked on an altar wasn't the best way of conducting an interrogation, but unable to help himself anyway. It wasn't just because of his job, he reminded himself: no, he genuinely cared about Ruben, wanted to help him, wanted to bring him even the smallest modicum of comfort. "Elias, why did he do it?"

"A diversion, apparently." Ruben's hands squeezed into fists and he swung around, misery shining from his eyes and anger in the set of his mouth. "A fucking diversion! That's all I am. I mean nothing to him. His son, his heir—and yet he cuts off my wings and send me into exile. How can he hate me so much?"

Victor didn't know what to say. "I'm sorry."

"And to trick me into almost killing you—you, who could be the one..."

"The one?" Victor repeated, puzzled. "What one?"

Ruben stopped, looking embarrassed. He rubbed at his eyes and dropped his head. "Uh, the one who saved me. From myself. From my hedonistic ways. You're so sensible, you see." His embarrassment seemed to increase, and Ruben turned away. "Anyway."

Confused, Victor echoed, "Anyway..."

Turning back to face him, Ruben said, "I'm not going to kill you. I'm not going to use you to regain my wings. Wait a moment and I'll untie you."

He crossed over to the pillar and with deft fingers, unfastened the knots holding the rope around Victor's ankles. Victor kicked off the bonds and bent his knees with a sigh of relief, his tail relaxing against his thigh. A moment later he felt the pressure in his arms loosen and he drew his hands down against his chest, free from the other set of ropes. "Thank you."

Ruben avoided his gaze. He hunted beneath one of the pews and pulled out a plastic bag. "Your clothes are in here. Sorry."

"Your feather." Victor lifted it from his chest and held it out, pushing it into Ruben's hand as he swapped it for the bag containing his clothes. He watched as Ruben stared at the feather with a mixture of sorrow and disgust before shoving it into his jeans pocket. "Elias, you should probably finish getting dressed, too."

"Huh? Oh, yeah." Ruben seemed to shake himself out of his reverie. He brushed past Victor and collected up his clothes, placing them on the altar and pulling on each garment. Victor smiled, envious of the way the angel dressed so untidily yet the overall effect was one of styled nonchalance.

When they were both clothed, Victor leaned against the altar. "Now what?"

Ruben shrugged. "Now you arrest me or something, I guess. Take me to the nearest DTM safe house for further questioning."

"No." Victor spoke without thought, but even after he'd said it, he knew he'd meant it. He didn't want Ruben imprisoned again. Even if he lost his position within the DTM hierarchy over this, even if he was demoted to a sixth rank demon—he wouldn't let Ruben be locked up.

Victor held out his hands, and Ruben took them. "We're in this together," Victor told him. "Your father has set you up for some reason, just as I believe my father—and possibly me—have also been set up. Someone's behind this. We need to find out who—and we need to put a stop to it."

* * *

Warm water poured down over Victor's body and steam fogged the panels of the shower cubicle. He worked shampoo into his hair then rinsed it out, the movements methodical while he considered the events of the last few days. All the pieces of the puzzle were coming together, but not as fast or coherently as he'd like.

Frowning, he adjusted the temperature with the mixer taps and made an involuntary sound of pleasure as the heat kicked up a notch. To Hell with it, he should really learn to switch off every now and then and just enjoy the situation. Forty-five minutes ago, he'd been tied up naked to the high altar in Rosslyn Chapel. Now he stood beneath a hot shower, washing with designer gels and shampoos, in the en-suite of one of the swankiest hotels in Edinburgh.

Ruben had paid for it, of course. He said it was his way of apologizing for drugging Victor and kidnapping him and subjecting him to the threat of death over a powerful ley line. Victor had allowed him to book the room, trying not to laugh out loud when he saw the names Ruben had used to sign them in: Ludwig Wiedemann and Mario-Ramon Diez.

"What shall we do now?" Victor had asked as soon as they'd arrived in their room overlooking one end of Princes Street. He admired the view of the castle perched high on its volcanic crag for a moment, then turned when Ruben's reply came out sounding muffled. "What did you say?"

"I said," Ruben repeated after he'd swallowed half of the complimentary chocolates, "you can do whatever you like. Tomorrow is soon enough for us to go chasing after master criminals."

Victor grinned beneath the spray of water at the memory. Master criminals, indeed! He supposed Ruben had a point, though—Barbosa Major had clearly put a lot of thought into disposing of his son. Chopping off Ruben's wings was a pretty big distraction, and if it was related to the Cape Verde plane crash and Valentin Tristan, then Victor believed they were teetering on the verge of uncovering something big.

And something that possibly—probably— implicated his father Valdemar.

Victor sighed and ducked his head under the

steady stream of water, squeezing his eyes shut. He felt the heat wash over him, soothing him, and relaxed further. A moment later, he heard the click of the cubicle door open and close, and felt Ruben's hard and very aroused body fit against him.

"You were taking too long. I just came to check you hadn't washed yourself down the plughole." Ruben gave him a sexy grin and reached past him for the shower gel. Squeezing some onto his palm, he rubbed the liquid across Victor's shoulders, lathering him up with strong, firm strokes.

Victor bit back a moan of pleasure and wrapped his tail, which had been hanging down between his thighs, tight around one leg.

Ruben purred. "You don't want me to soap your tail, buttercup?"

"I—I..." Victor glanced back at him, hesitated a second, then unwound his tail. "It's all yours."

The look of delight Ruben gave him was bright enough to light the entire city. "Really? You'll let me?"

Victor laughed, suddenly confident. He flicked back his hair and nodded. "You can play with my tail. I... I like it when it's touched near the base of my spine. And the tip—that's very sensitive."

Ruben poured half the contents of the shower gel onto his hand in his excitement. "It's like having two cocks to play with. Oh man. That's so hot."

Another laugh burst from Victor, but this time it was slightly ragged. Ruben reached down with the gel-covered hand and grasped Victor's tail, which unfurled and rose up, the pointed tip swaying at shoulder height. With his free hand, Ruben stroked across Victor's chest, rubbing the pads of his fingers over Victor's tight nipples. Darts of pleasure arrowed straight to his cock. He'd been half hard since Ruben had got into the shower with him, but now his erection surged to full strength.

Victor's legs trembled as he remembered Ruben's hot, wet mouth on him in the garden of the safe house. Coupled with the teasing of his nipples and the smooth stroking action on his tail, Victor's thoughts fragmented. He groaned, the sound echoing from the tiles. The beat of the shower spray against his face and chest seemed to mimic the deep, insistent pulse of desire inside him.

"Want me to slow this down?" Ruben asked, his voice husky in Victor's ear.

"Nn." Victor had temporarily forgotten how to speak. He took a breath. "No. Do whatever you like."

"Mm, I love it when you give me permission to do sexy, dirty things to your sexy, dirty body." Ruben nipped Victor's earlobe then took his tail in both hands. The left he wrapped around the base of Victor's tail where it joined his spine, and with the right he closed his fingers around the width of the tail and began to stroke it as if masturbating, moving upwards each time. His hand slid with ease over the slick length of Victor's tail, stimulating every inch of flesh.

"Oh God, Elias," Victor whispered, the words catching in his throat. "Don't stop."

"Not for a long time, buttercup." Ruben worked his hand up Victor's tail, circling it with his thumb and forefinger as the end tapered to a point. Holding the tip, he washed it clean of soapsuds then bent his head and ran his tongue over the point.

Victor squeaked and jerked forward, catching himself against the wall. As Ruben sucked and nibbled on his tail, Victor's mind clouded with pleasure. Orgasm built in a rush, his balls tucking up tight and his cock pulsing. It wouldn't take much. All he had to do was palm his erection and he'd come right there and then.

"Not yet," Ruben said as if reading his mind. He slipped his hand back down the length of Victor's tail, releasing his grasp on the base. Ruben stroked the dimples just above where the curve of the tail joined his body, then slid his fingers beneath the tail and down into the crease of Victor's arse.

Victor went still, his heart thudding with a mixture of excitement and curiosity. Ruben burrowed his fingers deeper, lower, until he rested the tip of his middle finger against Victor's hole. He pressed slightly and Victor jumped, giving a breathless laugh. It felt strange, possessive and invasive, but it made lust churn inside him.

"Relax." The command wrapped around him, and Victor murmured as Ruben pressed a little harder. "Breathe, buttercup. Take a deep breath for me. That's good. Another one. Let it go. Bear down on my finger. Yeah, like that..."

Ruben's smoky instructions were almost lost to the pounding of the spray and the rapid thump of Victor's pulse. He did as he was told, gasping as Ruben's finger pushed inside him past the resistance of muscle. Despite the warmth of the shower, Victor shivered, waves of hot and cold beating at him. He tilted his hips, pushing back against the intrusion, and moaned when he felt Ruben's finger slide all the way in.

"Good. That's good, baby." Ruben's voice sounded clipped with excitement. "God, I wish I had my cock inside you."

His words conjured up a picture of the two of them screwing, Ruben's cock buried deep inside Victor's arse. Victor sobbed for breath, leaning forward as Ruben began to finger-fuck him. He went slow at first, stretching his hole, then moved faster.

"Lift your tail," Ruben ordered, and Victor curled his tail back, lifting it straight against his spine. He heard Ruben growl, then felt him catch at the point of his tail with his mouth.

Victor yelled, his arse full of Ruben's finger and his

sensitive tail-tip between Ruben's lips. When Ruben nibbled on the edge of his tail, Victor lost control, thrusting back against him, impaling himself on Ruben's finger. A quiver racked his body, sensation spiraling, muscles tightening. He wanted to drop one hand and touch himself, bring himself off, but he didn't dare let go of the wall in case he fell down.

Gasping and crying aloud, Victor shuddered into a sudden, hard orgasm. He lifted his face to the spray, swallowing a mouthful of water before he came to his senses. While he still trembled, the aftershocks sending fresh spurts of come splashing against the tiles, Ruben gathered him close and held him.

Victor leaned back against Ruben, his heartbeat thundering as he gasped for breath. "That—that was..."

Ruben nuzzled through his wet hair and kissed Victor's neck. "Fantastic?" he suggested, leaning over to turn off the water.

"Fantastic." Victor managed to nod and speak at the same time. He swayed closer, his body slippery against Ruben's, and felt the hard thrust of Ruben's cock push at the curve of his arse. Feeling guilty, Victor tried to pull away. "You—what about you...?"

"I've had fun with your tail—now I get to play with the rest of you." Ruben gave him a filthy grin and pushed open the door of the shower cubicle. "Come with me, buttercup. That was just the starter."

Dazed, Victor stumbled out of the shower and caught the fluffy white towel Ruben threw at him. He patted down his body and rough-dried his hair, then followed the angel through into the bedroom. Ruben shed his towel before he reached the bed and leaned forward to drag the duvet from the mattress. He looked back over his shoulder and gave Victor an inviting smile.

"Nice big bed. Let's try it, shall we?"

Though he'd only just come, Victor felt his cock begin to rise again. Damn, what was it about Ruben that got him so hot? An ache started inside him. He wanted Ruben to fuck him again—not with his fingers this time, but with his big, hard cock. The thought made Victor whimper. He dropped his towel and hurried forwards, his gaze fixing on the wing stumps as they flexed with each movement Ruben made. The sight of them reminded Victor of the first day they'd met, of how Ruben had lounged half naked in the chair and how he'd responded so wonderfully when Victor had whispered close to his wing stumps...

Victor caught Ruben around the waist and together they toppled onto the sheets. Breathless with desire, Victor clambered on top of him, splaying his thighs to pin Ruben down. Ruben laughed and writhed beneath him, encouraging him to do whatever he wanted. Victor licked across Ruben's nape, then rearranged himself so he could touch the wing stumps.

Ruben realised what he was doing and went still. "Victor. Don't—don't touch them. I don't want you touching them. They're... they're ugly."

Victor shook his head. "Beautiful," he said. "They're beautiful."

With a muttered curse, Ruben tried to throw him off, but Victor clung tight and took one of the wing stumps between his lips.

The curse turned into a strangled sound, then into a sob. "Victor!"

Beneath his tongue, the wing stump flexed. Victor groaned, licking over the destroyed limb, tasting the ticklish down of tiny feathers and the sharper taste of Ruben's skin. The heat radiating from the angel was incredible, the water droplets from the shower drying in an instant and fresh sweat dewing his body. Ruben moaned helplessly, his shoulders hunching in reaction as Victor sucked on the wing stump while he caressed the other with the palm of his hand.

"You mustn't." Ruben sounded broken. "How can you even bear to look at them, let alone put your mouth on them?"

Victor lifted his head. "I love your wings."

"I don't have any wings!"

"You do. They're sexy. You're sexy." Victor kissed both wing stumps, feeling his heart fill with dizzying emotion. "I love you."

Ruben arched and squirmed. "Don't love me! I'm bad for you. I make a habit of seducing pretty blonds and then throwing them away when I get bored. That's not what you want, not what you need. I'm all wrong for you."

"I want you." Victor buried his face between the wing stumps and pressed an open-mouthed kiss to the center of Ruben's back. "I love you, Elias, and I'm not going to change my mind."

"Stubborn little demon!" Ruben managed to buck Victor off him.

Sprawled across the bed, Victor pushed his damp hair out of his eyes and smiled as Ruben crawled towards him. "Yes, I'm stubborn when I want something. And when I want something, I usually get it."

Ruben growled and swatted Victor's flank. "The only thing you're getting is a spanking."

Excitement shivered through him. Victor made his eyes very wide. "Promise?"

"Demon! I can't resist you." Ruben pounced, kissing Victor breathless. Their erections brushed together as they realigned their bodies into a more comfortable position, and then they rubbed and thrust against each other, thighs tangling and hands groping as they continued to kiss.

Ruben suddenly pulled away. "I want to be inside you, buttercup. Now."

Victor's breath caught in his throat. "I want it, too."

"Roll over for me. I want you on your hands and knees. Lift that sexy tail out of the way so I can get at you."

The command made Victor gasp. Pushing himself up, he caught a glimpse of their reflections in the mirrored doors of the wardrobe. He couldn't believe how he looked, naked and aroused, his cock dripping, his tail waving high above his head, his hair tangled in his face and his little red horns visible. He stared as Ruben knelt up behind him, an expression of dark, intense concentration on his face. Then Ruben noticed where he was looking and grinned.

"You like to watch, buttercup?"

It was on the tip of his tongue to tell Ruben that their exploits in the wood had been captured on camera, but he decided not to bother. It would be a secret for another day—and maybe, if they could discover the truth behind the Valentin Tristan affair, the DTM might hand over the tape to Victor. He purred at the thought of playing the tape in private for Ruben, so turned on by the fantasy of it that he almost didn't notice the feeling of something cool and liquid against his arsehole. Startled, he tried to pull away, focusing on their image in the mirror.

"Lube," Ruben said, holding up a gleaming finger. "I want to slip inside you nice and smooth." He slid the same finger into Victor's arse, spreading the gel, the touch making him quiver and strain forwards, his cock twitching with every tiny spasm. He cried out when Ruben withdrew, but seconds later Victor felt the head of Ruben's cock pressing against him.

Their gazes met in the mirror. Ruben gripped Victor's hips, holding him in place. "Breathe, sweetheart. Breathe and come back onto me."

Victor drew in a deep breath and eased backwards. At the same time, Ruben thrust into him. Victor felt a slight burn as his hole stretched to take the girth of Ruben's cock, but then he was deep inside, filling Victor completely.

The sensation was incredible, unlike anything he'd experienced or imagined. He hung there, impaled on Ruben's prick, gasping and gasping, his heart crashing against his ribs.

"Okay, buttercup?" Ruben's voice was warm and affectionate.

Victor realised Ruben was waiting for him. He nodded once. "I'm okay."

"You're more than okay. You feel like Heaven." Ruben began to move, taking it slow and steady, working in and out of Victor with a measured rhythm. He moaned when Victor flexed his arsehole, gripping onto his cock. "Victor. God. You're so fucking tight. And when you do that..."

A breathless laugh spilled from Victor's lips. "You like it?"

"More than anything." Ruben clutched tighter at one hip and moved his free hand forward to grasp at Victor's cock. "Can you balance on one hand and do it yourself? Can you jerk off while I fuck you? I'd like to see you do that, buttercup. I want us to watch ourselves in the mirror. I want you to see what you look like when you come with me inside you."

Victor whimpered, another orgasm building, the sensation sparkling around his tail and racing up his spine. He curled his tail, rubbing the sensitive point over the rough hair on Ruben's chest. They both groaned, and Ruben dragged Victor back onto his cock, gentle movements forgotten as he started to ride him with strong, powerful thrusts.

Keeping watch on their reflections, Victor balanced himself and reached down to grip his cock. He wrapped his fingers around the length and squeezed, panting for breath at the violent pleasure that glittered through him. He rubbed and stroked, matching his pace to Ruben's, and soon they were moving as one.

Ruben slammed into him, driving them onwards. Sweat stung Victor's eyes as he worked his cock and stared at the mirror. He didn't know where to look: at himself, his mouth wide and his lips soft, his cock fiercely dark and with pre-cum spooling from it, or at Ruben, fucking him from behind, his head thrown back and his chest gleaming with sweat as he pistoned in and out of Victor's body.

It was too much for him. The sight, the sound, the scent, the feeling—Victor cried out, his orgasm exploding through him, shaking him to the very core. His hole clenched, spasms rocking him again and again, milking Ruben's cock as he rode him. He heard Ruben yell, saw the blank look of ecstasy cross his face, was aware of the hot flood of spunk inside him. Victor juddered and jolted, his hips rocking, the tremors of the aftershocks pulsing more and more seed from his cock onto the sheets until he felt drained and exhausted, but utterly exhilarated.

His head swam as he struggled to force air into his lungs. Victor collapsed forward, his head on his arms, and lay still. Dimly he was aware of Ruben withdrawing from him and moving off the bed. Victor murmured in protest and tried to push himself up, feeling the trickle of semen down his thigh. He remained where he was until Ruben came back with a warm, damp washcloth and cleaned him up. Then they stretched out beside one another and rested.

It was Ruben who broke the lengthening silence. "We need to talk."

Victor stirred and rolled over to look at him. "About what?"

Ruben fidgeted with a corner of the duvet, then

pulled it up over their naked bodies. "About us. I mean, about what we should do." Words seemed to desert him. "About what we should do tomorrow."

The burgeoning panic inside him died down, and Victor gave a discreet sigh of relief. He had no desire to be given the brush-off after the best sex of his life—especially not after he'd told Ruben he loved him. Maybe that had been a bit premature, but Victor didn't care. Of course, it would have been better if Ruben had reciprocated, but still... Victor refused to give up just yet.

"One of my yachts is at berth in Sitges, near Barcelona," Ruben said. "I could make a call and have the crew bring it to France, somewhere just north of the DTM/FIA border. With the second half of the dual spell-cast Raul and Isaac gave me, we'll be able to hop over to France and then take my yacht to Spain, where we can begin the search for Valentin..."

Victor frowned and sat up. "Raul and Isaac?" The names rang a bell.

"Raul Soler and Isaac Bertram," Ruben said helpfully. "Raul is an ex-angel and Isaac's an ex-demon. Actually, Isaac still seemed pretty demonic to me, even though they're both human now. My father sent Raul to seduce Isaac in—"

"Switzerland," Victor interrupted, staring at him. "The Head of Station H mentioned them to me a week or so ago when I first arrived in Finland. I think it was meant as a warning for me not to do the same thing as Isaac."

Ruben wrinkled his nose. "Lose your wings?"

"Fall in love with an angel." Victor sighed. "I don't have any wings yet. Maybe I won't ever get any wings, especially with all this business seemingly connected to my father. It all adds up, Elias—Valentin, your father, the black market coffee smuggling, my father, the photos of you, me being brought into this case..."

"We need to go to Spain." Ruben curled one arm around Victor and tried to pull him down onto the bed. "C'mon, buttercup. I'll be offended if you don't go to sleep. I pride myself on shagging my pretty blonds senseless, and you have far too much sense right now."

Victor cuddled close to him. "Sex with you makes me feel alive. Awake. Inspired."

Ruben groaned and hid his head under a pillow. "Be inspired tomorrow," he said, his voice muffled. "Tomorrow, we'll go to Spain. I have friends in high places my father doesn't know about. We'll track down Valentin and sort this out once and for all."

"No," Victor said, the decision crystallizing in his mind. "We need to know what we're getting into, and I need clear answers. Before we search for Valentin, we need to go to Monaco. We need to see my father."

CHAPTER 11

Victor stood on the wide balcony of the Resident's house and breathed in the warm, salty air borne on the breeze. Below him lay the marina, the lights aboard the yachts and cruisers at their berths twinkling like fallen stars in contrast to the glitz and sparkle of the Monte Carlo seafront. The sound of the waves almost drowned out the noise of a crowd of revelers heading towards the nightclub zone.

A sense of familiarity made Victor relax, even though he knew Monaco wasn't a safe place. Nowhere in the DTM was safe for him at the moment, he was sure of it, not until he and Ruben had got to the bottom of this business with Valentin Tristan.

He sighed and tipped his head back against the wall, closing his eyes for a moment. He tightened his fingers around the mug of coffee the housekeeper had given him and wondered when his father would be home. The housekeeper had said any time after six o'clock. It was gone seven now.

They'd arrived just outside of Monte Carlo on the winding road that snaked down from the hills. Ruben had apologized for the landing—"The spell-cast must be faulty, I was aiming for the marina!"—but there was nothing else they could do but walk the last few miles into the city. At least it was downhill all the way. Victor didn't think he could deal with anything more strenuous, not after the explosive and exhaustive night and morning of sex he'd shared with Ruben. His tail tingled and he could swear his horns had grown. In fact, his entire body felt new and ripe, as if something had changed inside him.

When he'd asked Ruben if he looked different, the angel studied him with a leer and said, "You look thoroughly fucked. Is that what you mean, buttercup?"

Victor hadn't bothered to ask him again. Sometimes it really wasn't worth it.

Now he lifted the mug to his lips and took a sip of coffee. The blandness of the decaffeinated brew made him grimace. Coffee in Monaco was even more strictly regulated than in the UK, partly because of the principality's location. Since it was surrounded by FIA territory, demons visiting Monaco always assumed they'd be able to gain access to high quality black market goods. Valdemar tried hard to dispel this assumption, which was one of the reasons why it was considered such an awful place. In addition, demons disliked warm, sunny weather, but Victor had grown up here and he saw nothing wrong with Monaco's climate or the range of goods on offer in the shops. As his father's place of exile, it had a lot to recommend it.

A few more gulps of coffee and Victor couldn't stand it any longer. He crossed the balcony and tipped the remainder of the drink over the side into the garden. Setting the mug on the wide railing, he leaned forwards on his elbows and stared at the Mediterranean. Weariness washed over him. He hadn't slept much last night, unaccustomed to sharing bed space with anyone, let alone a highly-sexed angel, and after their forced march into the city, Victor was ready to turn in. He'd left Ruben dozing on the elegant leather couch in Valdemar's formal sitting room, but until his father returned home, Victor didn't want to go to sleep.

A faint sound within the room made him turn. He jumped, his pulse racing, then frowned, reminding himself they were safe within the Residence. Collecting his mug, he went back indoors.

Ruben sat bolt upright on the couch, his hands pressed in his lap and a bright, nervous smile on his face as he stared at the man on the other side of the room. Without looking in Victor's direction, he said in an over-loud voice, "Victor! Your father is here! Isn't that great!"

Victor glanced over at Valdemar, who stood glowering at Ruben. "Hi, Dad."

"Good evening, son. It seems you've brought a... friend." Valdemar flicked his gaze away from Ruben and looked at Victor, finally breaking into a smile. "Come and give your old man a hug."

Putting down the coffee mug, Victor went over to his father and embraced him. Valdemar held him back by the shoulders. "You look different."

Victor blushed and tried hard not to glance in Ruben's direction.

"Well." Valdemar let him go and gestured to the couch. "Sit with your friend and tell me why I have the pleasure of your company."

As Victor took a seat, Ruben skittered across the couch and sat close. Surprised by the angel's reaction, he glanced over and saw Ruben hunched into himself, his eyes wide as he stared at Valdemar's tattered dark blue demon wings. "First rank demon?" he whispered to Victor.

"Second rank, upper class." Valdemar strolled across the room to a small bar hidden inside a bureau. "Either of you boys want a drink? Brandy? Scotch? Vodka?"

They shook their heads. Victor began, "Dad, this is Ruben—"

"Ruben Patrick Barbosa Minor, son of Barbosa Major, Controller South of the FIA." Valdemar poured a generous amount of brandy into a cut glass tumbler. "I know who he is... and I know where he should be right now. Where you both should be right now, but let's forget about that for the moment. Why are you here?"

Victor and Ruben exchanged looks. Valdemar sat opposite them in a leather wing-chair, the glass of brandy placed on a small table beside him. From his suit jacket pocket he took out a cigar and a book of matches and proceeded to light up. "Come on, boys, I haven't got all night. I've just come back from a very dull gala dinner in honor of an exceedingly tedious politician who retired here twenty years ago. My brain wishes to shut down, so unless you start talking soon, you'll have to wait until tomorrow."

"We can wait until tomorrow, sir," Ruben said, quivering with tension.

"No, we can't," Victor said. "Dad doesn't wake up until two in the afternoon. We need to be on our way as soon as possible."

Valdemar puffed on his cigar. "A flying visit, is it?"

Taking a deep breath, Victor launched into their story. He told his father about the interrogations in Turku, omitting certain details irrelevant to the case, and explained about the connection between Ruben and Valentin Tristan. He mentioned setting off the alarm after hacking the DTM mainframe, brought in Ruben's job as a coffee nose and blender, and made discreet but pointed reference to the black market coffee-smuggling rings within DTM territory. By the end of his speech, he was sitting on the edge of the couch, his body taut as he waited for his father's reaction.

"I scc." Valdemar drew the cigar from his mouth and, holding it between thumb and forefinger, examined the lit end. He looked up at Victor through a veil of smoke. "Where do I fit in?"

Victor felt the words freeze in his throat. He couldn't accuse of his father of betraying the DTM. What proof did he have? It was all conjecture. And yet—and yet... He squared his shoulders and met Valdemar's gaze. "That's what I want to know. Do you fit in, Dad? Valentin Tristan was one of our coffee scientists here in Monaco. He went over to the FIA. He couldn't have done it without high-level help. Defecting from Monaco five years ago would have been almost impossible. The place was run by the angels then! I remember it, Dad—I remember how it used to be to live here. Every time I wanted to visit you for the holidays, I had to fill out twelve forms in triplicate. It took sixteen forms for me to leave to go back to university! Any demon passing in or out of Monte Carlo was tagged and watched. Humans who worked for us had it just as hard. So how did Valentin make the jump?"

Valdemar clamped his teeth around the cigar. "It happens. People make mistakes."

"No!" Victor sprang to his feet, his hands curling into fists. He shook off Ruben's restraining grasp and stalked over to his father. "No, Dad. I don't believe it. Why have you been the Monaco Resident for so long?"

"Maybe I like it here." Valdemar smiled, but it didn't touch his eyes.

"Cut the crap! Dad, I know something's going on. I'm involved in it. Elias is involved in it. And you're involved in it—and whatever it is, it stinks. It stinks almost as much as the bullshit you're giving me now."

For a moment silence weighed heavily around the room, and then Valdemar stubbed out his cigar and took a long sip from his brandy. He sat back in his chair and steepled his fingers, regarding Victor with a faintly amused expression. "Well, now. I always thought I'd raised you better than to go around shouting and swearing."

Victor felt his face redden. "Sorry."

"Sit down, son."

Ruben tugged on Victor's arm and he sat, his gaze never wavering from his father. "The truth, Dad. I want the truth."

Valdemar nodded. "And you will have it." He waved a hand around at the room. "After twenty years as Resident, I know this is probably the safest place in Monaco in which to have a sensitive conversation. Listen to me, both of you—for this concerns you too, Ruben—and try not to interrupt.

I'm tired and I want to go to bed soon."

Victor flicked a sidelong glance at Ruben, who looked bewildered by Valdemar's bombastic approach. Nevertheless, they both remained silent as Valdemar finished his brandy and set down the empty glass on the table with a heavy thud.

"You're right. This business is connected to coffee and the black market." An amused smile curved Valdemar's mouth. "You've got good instincts, kid. Didn't I tell you to trust in your instincts? Anyway—for years now, the DTM has been concerned about the FIA monopoly on coffee. There's a trade agreement in place that restricts the amount of raw and processed coffee permitted to cross the borders. On paper, the angels only send what we demons consume. There's no coffee surplus mountain hidden away in a warehouse outside Brussels, as some like to claim. No, we drink x-amount of gallons of the stuff and that's precisely the amount of beans and blended powder that the FIA sends."

Victor looked at Ruben again, and Ruben nodded. "That's right."

Valdemar frowned at him. "Of course I'm right. Where was I? Oh, yes. For a long time now, over a decade, the DTM has worried what would happen if the FIA reneged on the agreement. What would happen if the angels stopped the supply? Caffeine is the demon drug of choice, and while its consumption is monitored by the government, it's considered safe. If the supply stops, demons will turn to the black market for their fix, robbing the treasury of valuable caffeine tax and also ensuring that the demon population becomes out of control and doped to the eyeballs.

"That brings me to the other concern put forward by the DTM. How can we trust the FIA? What if they tamper with the coffee and flood the market with dangerous blends, either through legal channels or via the black market?"

Ruben leaned forward. "Excuse me, sir, but that fear is justified. Some of the blends I worked on before my father ordered me away from the job were specifically designed to deliver a high impact yield of caffeine in a very small shot—kind of like a super-hyper-charged espresso."

"Indeed?" Valdemar sat a little straighter and gazed at him with interest. "Hmm, such information could be useful. I don't suppose you'd be prepared to go into more detail tomorrow when I can assemble our coffee scientists?"

"I..." Ruben turned to Victor, his expression troubled. "Should I?"

"Yes." Victor spoke without hesitation. "You're not betraying your people, Elias. You've seen already how demons react to coffee. How I react to it." He blushed and continued, "And I'm sure you can imagine what would happen if the effect was magnified by five or tenfold... It would cause mass insanity and death. You don't want your nose to be used to create a biological weapon, do you?"

A look of horror paled Ruben's face. He covered his nose and shook his head.

"Good, that's settled." Valdemar rubbed his hands together. "I'll arrange for you to meet our scientists first thing tomorrow morning. We've been running some tests on a recent batch of black market coffee seized by German police in the Rhineland, and found traces of genetic manipulation. Your input will be invaluable."

Victor blinked. "So you know about the smuggling ring."

"It's flown into Berlin Schönefeld and redistributed. Yes, we know." Valdemar flashed him an unreadable look. "We also know about Ludwig Wiedemann's preference for a certain Colombian brew. Oh yes, we know. But it's better for us to pretend we don't know and permit the black market to continue under our watchful gaze than attempt to shut it down and risk it springing up like a many-headed hydra elsewhere across DTM territory where we can't monitor it."

"That seems to make sense." Victor hadn't considered that. "So the black market smuggling is state sanctioned?"

"In effect."

Conscious that his father had deviated from the

original subject, Victor tried to steer the conversation back on track. "Where does Valentin Tristan come into all this, Dad? I know he's a coffee scientist, a human... And why were his files in the 'deleted personnel' section of the DTM mainframe?"

Valdemar blew out a breath. He edged his chair closer towards the couch and lowered his voice, as if afraid of being overheard even here in the safest room in Monaco. "Valentin's defection was staged. I arranged it myself." He paused, then added, "I'm his case officer."

Victor stared, his thoughts jumbled. "Then this is all..."

"Valentin's a sleeper agent." Valdemar smiled again, though this time there was weariness and worry behind it.

Ruben snorted. "Sleeper agent. That's funny." He tilted his head to stare at Valdemar. "You do know he was sleeping with my friend Marc Soto?"

Valdemar nodded. "Yes. That was part of his job."

"Marc loves him!" Ruben bounced off the couch, anger radiating from him. Beneath his loose shirt, his wing stumps twitched. "Marc is good and kind. He doesn't deserve to be tricked like this!"

"Sit down, Barbosa Minor." Valdemar pointed at the couch. "Sit down."

Ruben stopped mid-tirade and sat down meekly.

"When Monaco was controlled by the angels," Valdemar began, "I was permitted to stay here as Resident. There were no complicated reasons—just an acknowledgement that the principality had run well with me in charge in the past, so my continued presence seemed to make sense to both the DTM and FIA." He looked at Victor. "I was approached by Joseph Cabrera about switching sides and joining the angels. I told him I wasn't interested. At the same time, the Director-General of the DTM gave me an order to find out as much as possible about the FIA's coffee plans.

"Since I'd already turned down Cabrera's offer, it would have looked suspicious if I made contact again saying I'd changed my mind. Instead, I decided to send in a man I knew I could trust implicitly— Valentin Tristan."

Ruben scowled and muttered until Victor elbowed him in the ribs.

Valdemar continued: "Perhaps you remember, Victor—Monte Carlo was party central in those days. When I heard that the Rio Resident was paying a visit with the FIA's Controller South, I knew I had to take the chance. Valentin is a brilliant coffee scientist, the best the DTM has ever produced, so I allowed him to mingle with his colleagues at a party to welcome Soto and Barbosa Major. Though I knew Valentin would technically be working for Barbosa Major, he'd have most contact with Soto, who's involved in the legal side of FIA coffee export. So I put Valentin in Soto's path and that was it." He sighed. "At first it was purely business between them. But now..."

"Now Marc loves him," Ruben growled.

"Now that feeling is mutual," Valdemar said. He shook his head. "Valentin reported back to me every month, and I re-encrypted the information and sent it on to London. Only myself, Valentin, and the Director-General knew about this operation. My apparent fall from grace over the last few years was a ruse the Director-General set in place to enable me to stay here and monitor Valentin's progress."

"Except that progress seems to have stalled," Victor said, laying a soothing hand on Ruben's knee before the angel could get angry again. "Why was Valentin flying to Spain?"

Valdemar stared at his empty glass. "He wanted out. Things were getting too hot for him in Brazil. He thought he was being watched by government agents, and his relationship with Marc had taken an unexpected turn. Valentin was in love, and he knew that if suspicion fell on him, Marc would be dragged into it. FIA interrogations are not like ours, Victor. They're much more brutal. Barbosa Major would have no problem torturing both Valentin and Marc to get a confession."

Victor looked at Ruben, who nodded and bowed his head. "It's true. I've seen the things my father does to prisoners. He likes causing pain."

Victor put an arm around Ruben and gave him a brief hug. Looking at his father, he asked, "Where is Valentin now?"

Valdemar opened his hands palm upwards, a look of frustration on his face. "I don't know. Part of the deal I had with Valentin was that if he wanted out, he'd book a flight to Spain on the pretext of visiting his family. As soon as he defected to the FIA, they took his family into protective custody and set them up in a place in Barcelona to ensure Valentin's good behaviour. But there's a lot of loopholes in Spanish law, loopholes we can use to get Valentin and his family out if the necessity arose."

"Except he didn't make it to Spain," Ruben said quietly. "His plane crashed over the Cape Verde Islands. I know. I saw it."

"And yet there's no record of a plane crash at those coordinates," Victor added. "Not from the DTM and not from the FIA."

Ruben looked up. "And then there's me. My own father cut off my wings and spell-cast me into the most northern country he could think of as a diversion. But for what?"

Valdemar looked at them both. "I can only imagine you were a diversion to cover up for the fact that there was no plane crash."

Victor and Ruben exchanged glances.

"I know," Valdemar continued, "that doesn't make any sense. And yet it's true. It's a master-stroke of simplicity. Ruben, your appearance in Finland caused a buzz of interest and speculation right across the DTM. You were the only one to mention this plane crash, which led to hundreds of agents across demon-controlled Europe searching for that specific plane over the last few days. We even sent agents to the crash site, hoping to find debris. But there's nothing there. The only logical conclusion, then, is..."

"Is that the plane never crashed, and Ruben was a double diversion," Victor finished, cold anxiety creeping into his belly. "Where do you think Valentin is now? Could Barbosa Major have turned the plane around after he'd attacked Elias? Is it possible that Valentin is back in Brazil?"

Silence stretched around them, and then Ruben stood. "I will call Marc and talk to him. I will ask him if he knows of Valentin's whereabouts."

"No." Valdemar shook his head. "We don't want to warn the angels that anything's amiss. If Marc is an innocent party to this plot, he could only make things worse. But if he's a part of it..."

"He's not." Ruben sounded absolutely certain.

Valdemar heaved a deep sigh. "If you want my opinion, boys, I believe Valentin is in Spain. I think the plane rerouted, changed its tags, and landed at a civilian airport in plain sight. But in order to prove my suspicion—and to rescue Valentin—I need someone willing to go into the FIA."

For a moment Victor held his breath. He glanced at Ruben, who nodded slightly, then said, "That's what we wanted to do, Dad. Spain seemed to be the logical place to start looking for Valentin."

"You need to avoid ports and airports." Valdemar ticked off the points on his fingers. "You'll need cash and false papers, just in case you're stopped. Victor, you'll need to style your hair to hide your horns. Steer clear of any DNA scanners, otherwise you'll both be arrested..."

Victor listened with amusement, realizing that his father was giving them orders even though they hadn't agreed to carry out the mission. He hid a grin. Wasn't this what he'd always wanted—the chance of being a real field agent? He just hadn't expected to go on a job alongside an angel.

"I have a yacht," Ruben told Valdemar. "It's not as flashy or sophisticated as the ones you photographed me on a couple of weeks ago—"

Valdemar grimaced. "Sorry about that, lad. Orders from the top. We thought by watching you, we might get some inkling of what your father was planning."

"My father doesn't tell me anything." Ruben's voice was brittle. He lifted his chin and continued, "I've given orders for my crew, who are all handpicked and trustworthy, to come here tomorrow morning. We'll sail to Sitges. I've got a berth there. I've got crews on stand-by for every yacht I own, and I make sure the boats are sailed often, so port personnel are used to my people coming and going. There shouldn't be any problems from the authorities. Victor and I will be able to get into Barcelona with ease."

Victor gave the angel an admiring look. Ruben glanced back at him with a brief smile. "Not just a pretty face, am I?"

"No, you're not." His voice came out husky, and Victor coughed, embarrassed.

"Then it's all settled." Valdemar looked pleased as he got to his feet. "If only all my problems were solved quite as simply. But now..." He turned to Ruben and managed a polite smile. "I'd like to speak with my son in private. If you'll excuse us?"

"Oh, sure. Yeah. I'll..." Ruben blushed and motioned towards the door.

"The housekeeper will show you the way," Victor said, not wanting to say out loud that he and Ruben were sharing a room. Valdemar would find out eventually, but he didn't want to have that conversation with his father just yet.

He watched as Ruben solemnly shook hands with Valdemar before he left the room, pulling the heavy oak door shut behind him. They listened to Ruben's footsteps fade across the parquet floor of the hallway, and then silence fell.

Victor smiled as he searched for something to say to break the slightly strained atmosphere between them. Valdemar studied him with interest, a frown wrinkling his brow as he took out another cigar and prepared to light it.

"You've changed," Valdemar said at length around the unlit cigar.

"I have?" Victor felt his stomach flip with nervous tension.

"Yes." The smell of sulphur hung briefly in the air as Valdemar struck a match. He shook out the flame and tossed the spent match aside, then puffed on his cigar for a few moments longer. "And it's not just because you've slept with Barbosa Minor, either."

"Dad!" An embarrassed blush climbed to his face. Victor brushed back his hair, his fingers touching one of his horns. A crackle of awareness, like an electric shock, zinged through him and he gasped, swaying forward.

Valdemar grabbed Victor before he could fall. "I was right. You have changed." There was pride in his voice, but also annoyance tinged with anxiety.

"What's happening to me?" Victor clutched at his father's arm and straightened up, still feeling the after-effects of the touch. "This only began today, after we'd landed here from the spell-cast. I thought it was because Elias and I were—because we'd—"

"It's not caused by sex." Valdemar patted his son's back, then rubbed across his shoulder blades as if looking for something. "Your wings are about to grow. Soon you'll be a second rank demon."

Victor pulled away from him. "What?"

"It's true. The tingling, the slight discomfort... it's time. Your wings are going to grow in the next couple of weeks."

"When?" Victor looked over his shoulder as if he could see his wings sprout through his shirt. "How long does it take? Will it hurt?"

Valdemar shrugged. "That's the problem. It's impossible to know for certain exactly when your wings will appear. It could be tomorrow—or it could be in two weeks." A shadow of concern darkened his expression. "The timing couldn't be worse. If your wings grow when you're in FIA territory..."

Victor stood straight. "I'm not afraid."

"No," said Valdemar, "but I am. You're my son, my only child. I'm so proud of you, Victor. If I lost you..."

"Dad. It'll be okay." Victor hugged his father. "Elias and I will do it. We'll find Valentin. And if my wings grow, I'll think of something. You know me— I'm resourceful."

Valdemar gave a crack of dry laughter. "That you are. Now then..." He stepped away from the embrace and returned to his cigar. "You do realise there's an alert out for you and Barbosa Minor from both Station H and from London Central."

"I thought there might be." Victor slid his hands into his back pockets and leaned against the side of the couch. "They must know I'd come to you."

"I've received no direct orders. Until I do..."

"Thanks, Dad."

They stood in silence for a while, Valdemar smoking his cigar and Victor listening to the sound of the sea through the open balcony windows.

At length Valdemar said, "Barbosa Minor. You love him."

Startled by his father's direct approach, Victor tried to prevaricate. "I don't know."

"That means yes." Valdemar's smile was gentle. "You've always been so certain about everything in life before."

Victor turned his head so his father couldn't read his expression. Hell, it was bad enough that Valdemar guessed they were screwing, but to admit to being in love with Ruben—he couldn't do it. Not yet, not when there was so much at stake. And it wasn't just the business with Valentin, either. "He's an angel."

"I didn't say it would be easy. Besides, when have you ever wanted things easy?"

"Dad." Victor scuffed his feet over the patterned rug on the floor then looked up. "It's not simply the angel thing. His father... I mean, Elias is more than an average angel. And he's a player. God, you took the surveillance photos yourself, you know how many guys he's had. I might be his type physically, but I think I only have novelty value for him. Just another in a long line."

"You assume a lot," Valdemar said softly.

Victor ignored the comment. "I don't know what to do."

"Are you just whining or are you asking for my advice?"

A grimace pulled at Victor's mouth. "Both."

"First of all, quit whining." Valdemar stubbed out his cigar half-smoked. "Secondly, listen to your old man. Don't make a decision now. Go to Spain with Barbosa Minor and find Valentin..."

"Yeah. The mission must always come first." Victor couldn't keep the trace of bitterness from his voice.

Valdemar raised his eyebrows and tutted. "Don't

get smart. Just do as I say. Things will fall into place."

Victor gave him a level look. "How can you be so sure?"

Valdemar smiled. "Because there's nothing better than terrible, life-threatening danger to bring two people together."

CHAPTER 12

"What are we doing here?"

Ruben glanced at Victor, who was dressed in a pair of old denim cut-offs and a grey t-shirt worn beneath a white cotton shirt, all of which Ruben had dug out from a cupboard on board his yacht. Victor looked hot, which was the whole point of the outfit, but he also looked annoyed, which wasn't what Ruben had intended. As he watched, Victor tapped his foot against the pavement and glared at him.

Adjusting the angle of his sunglasses, Ruben turned back to the pretty ice cream vendor and took the triple-scoop cone the girl held out. He paid and wandered off across the sunlit square towards the cathedral with Victor trailing after him.

"Elias..."

Ruben licked the ice cream and sighed with

delight. Pistachio, rum n' raisin and lavender-honey. Delicious. Not quite as delicious as licking Victor, but since they were in a public place, the ice cream was a good substitute.

"Ruben!" Victor grabbed his arm. A blob of ice cream dropped from the cone and splattered on the ground. They both looked down. "Sorry," Victor muttered, not sounding sorry in the slightest.

"If you wanted a lick, you only had to ask." Ruben offered him the cone. "The pistachio is really good."

Victor flushed an angry red. "We're supposed to be doing a job."

"I'm doing it. But first, I want ice cream." Ruben nibbled at the edge of one of the cones. "Even the wafer is good. Sugar-coated. Really fattening. I have great metabolism, though, so you don't need to worry that you'll wake up one day next to a fat bastard."

"Elias, I really think we should—" Victor stopped, a stunned expression on his face. "What did you just say?"

Ruben mouthed at the lavender and honey scoop and almost froze his lips. "Mmf. I said the wafer has sugar-coating and..."

Victor waved his hand. "Not that. The bit about you not becoming a fat bastard."

"It's true. I won't be." Ruben looked at him. "Were

you worrying that I would? You're so shallow, buttercup."

"That's not what I meant." Victor dropped his gaze and seemed to shrink a little.

Ruben regarded him with a frown, puzzled by what he could have said to cause such a reaction. Then he shrugged inwardly and carried on demolishing the ice cream. "Hey," he said in between crunching the remnants of the cone, "not that way. We're going in here."

Victor paused in the shadow of the cathedral and looked at the medieval stone-built house on the street behind them. The doorway opened into a small courtyard, tiled on all sides, with a fountain playing in the center of the square. Ruben finished eating, wiped his hands on the back of his jeans, and stepped into the courtyard.

"The city archives?" Victor whispered, entering the courtyard after him. "What, you think you'll find Valentin in here? This place looks ancient!"

"Fourteenth century," Ruben replied. "Didn't you read the guidebook? I left it out on the bed for you."

Victor blushed. "I didn't see it. Maybe it fell on the floor when we—"

"Just kidding." Ruben flashed him a huge smile. "I love teasing you, buttercup."

"Yes. Well." His blush deepening, Victor glanced around the tiled courtyard. A wisteria grew up an external staircase leading to a balcony and trailed over the wings of the building. Victor seemed very interested in the plant and refused to meet Ruben's gaze. "I suppose it's not a bad idea, coming here. Maybe we can search for Valentin's family. The city archives will have an address, right? We can visit his family and..."

"We'll be able to find help here," Ruben said.

Victor glanced at him. "You sound sure."

"I'm very sure." Taking off his sunglasses, Ruben headed for the old wood-and-iron door set into a recess in the main part of the building. "Come on. The quicker we do this, the quicker we can get back to the yacht and fun things."

"Fun things." Victor sighed. "Fun things like watching your crew go octopus fishing?"

"Not quite what I had in mind, but yeah, why not?" Ruben pushed open the door and led the way down an empty corridor. "I didn't know the guys went fishing from my yacht when I wasn't using it, but that's okay. You have to admit the calamari we had last night tasted pretty good."

"Your yacht looks more like a fishing trawler," Victor grumbled. "So many nets lying around, it's a trip hazard. And there're so many crewmen on board..."

"Oh, so it's not about the octopus, it's about the crew. I see." They came to another door, this one made of reinforced steel. Ruben paused in front of it while he flipped through his wallet for the appropriate card. He wiggled his eyebrows at Victor. "You don't like us having an audience when we go to bed."

Another adorable blush burned its way across Victor's face. "They can't help but overhear us! Especially when you won't even let us actually get to a bed in the privacy of a cabin before you start... doing what you do. This morning we were on the bow deck! Anyone could have seen!"

Ruben swiped the card in the lock device on one side of the door and waited for the light to flash green. "That's the point, buttercup. I want everyone to know just how hot and sexy and desirable I find you."

"You do?" Victor followed him through the steel door and down a narrow flight of stairs. Only when they reached another steel door at the bottom did he say, "Elias, where the Hell are we?"

Ruben turned the card over in his hand and hesitated for a moment. He put his back to the door and looked at Victor, hoping he'd done the right thing by coming here. Taking a deep breath, he asked, "Do you trust me?"

The pause seemed endless, and Victor looked bewildered. "Yes," he said. "Yes, Elias, I trust you."

"Good." Ruben let out the breath he'd been holding and lifted the card. "Don't get mad, okay?"

Victor stared at him, his expression even more confused. "Why? What have you done?"

Before he could change his mind, Ruben swiped the card through the lock and stepped aside as the door swung open. He took hold of Victor's arm and pulled him into the suite of rooms that lay beyond, but waited until the door clicked shut behind them before he said, "This is the Barcelona headquarters of the FIA. I'm sorry, Victor."

He watched the colour drain from Victor's face. The demon swayed on his feet then stood tall, lifting his chin. He shot Ruben a contemptuous glance. "I see. Was this your plan all along? Hand me over to the FIA in exchange for—for..."

Ruben rolled his eyes. "For what, exactly? My wings? Shit, buttercup, if I wanted my wings back so badly I'd have fucked you on that ley line and killed you!"

Victor scowled at him. "Then why are we here, if not to interrogate me?"

"Don't be so dramatic. We're here to get information, like I said."

"You won't get anything from me!" Victor squashed back against the wall, defiance in his eyes.

Ruben sighed. He'd done this all wrong. Maybe he should've told Victor where they were going, but he'd known that the demon wouldn't have agreed. Better to just trick him into it, like he'd done with the ley line. Okay, that hadn't worked out too well either, but not for want of trying. So he just had to try harder now. Victor was smart. He'd get it in the end, even if Ruben had to spell it out to him.

"I don't want anything from you. Actually I do, but that's purely on a personal level." Ruben gave him a winsome smile, but Victor just glared at him. Ruben tried again. "Okay, look—this is the FIA HQ. If anyone knows where Valentin is, it'll be them. Your dad thought he was being held here—so let's find out."

"We can't just walk in there and ask!" Victor flapped his hands.

"Why the Hell not? It's what I'm going to do." Ruben grabbed Victor's hand before he could start flailing again and towed him towards one of the rooms. "We'll start in here. Leave everything to me."

Victor mumbled something that sounded distinctly uncomplimentary, but allowed himself to be manhandled into the room.

Across a wide wooden desk, two angels rose to their feet, their wings lifted and bristling in curious welcome. Ruben glanced at the first, a young man barely out of his teens with stunning blue eyes and heavy brows, then focused on the second, a sweet-faced creature who stood staring wide-eyed and startled, his peregrine-coloured wings quivering with sudden tension.

Ruben grinned. This would be easier than he thought. "Hello, Marc."

* * *

Man, he rocked. Ruben stretched out on the Egyptian cotton sheets of the king-size bed that dominated the master cabin of the yacht and sighed with pleasure. Not only was he a red-hot lover, he'd also solved the mystery of Valentin's disappearance with minimal effort. Sure, he'd had that frisson of stress with Victor when they'd first gone into the FIA base beneath the Barcelona city archives, but that had only made sex all the sweeter. He really should rile Victor up more often.

The boat rocked gently at its mooring, the movement almost imperceptible. Ruben gave another happy sigh. He loved a good, slow fuck on water. It was better with big waves slapping the hull, of course, but the languorous dip and lift of the washes from passing boats had been just as much fun when he'd been buried inside Victor. He rolled onto his side, unsticking himself from the sheets, and looked at his demon lover. Ruben couldn't resist a smile of delight. He'd really hit the jackpot with this one. Pretty, blond, clever... and a demon.

Ruben's smile faded. Shit. He shouldn't think of the differences between them. He certainly shouldn't think about the look of suspicious anger on Valdemar Bischoff's face when they'd first met. Before Victor had come in from the balcony, Valdemar had told Ruben exactly what he thought of angels courting demons. Not impossible, he'd said—merely stupid. And Victor wasn't stupid. Oh, he might say he was in love now, but in the long term? Ruben knew he was fooling himself. Victor was a good little demon, the poster boy for good little demons, and good little demons didn't throw away the chance of rapid promotion and hometown glory for fantastic sex and a cheeky grin.

Thank God he'd never told Victor how close he was to falling in love with him. That would have been a disaster of epic proportions.

Victor stirred beside him, his blond hair ruffled and streaked dark with sweat. The tips of his horns showed red, and his tail flicked lazily back and forth on top of the tangled sheets. He smiled. "This was a good day."

Ruben grinned. "Every day is a good day with me, buttercup. Solving unsolvable problems—simple! Having four hours of amazing sex—piece of cake!"

"Cake." The look of affection in Victor's eyes was replaced by one of hunger. "I could do with a piece of cake. Need to keep up my strength."

"No cake, sorry. There's octopus."

Victor wrinkled his nose and cuddled closer. "I'll

do without, thanks."

Warm satisfaction spread through Ruben. He'd never wanted to snuggle like this with any of his other pretty blond boys, but with Victor it felt right. Comfortable. He sighed. "Now you can tell me how awesome I am for going to the FIA."

Tilting his head, Victor kissed the corner of Ruben's mouth. "You're awesome. But..." he continued, rolling back to put a slight distance between them, "you're also incredibly lucky that Marc was there."

Ruben shrugged. "Not luck, more like a really good guess. I knew how much Marc valued Valentin. It made sense that if there was a plane crash—or rumours of a plane crash—and an arrest, Marc would do everything in his power to free Valentin. Especially if it meant putting my father's nose out of joint. They might be in the coffee plantation business together, but my father's double-dealing and methods of persuasion are not universally liked."

"Tell me the truth, you called Marc from my dad's place, didn't you?" Victor lay on his front and propped his chin on his hands, blowing the tendrils of hair from his eyes. "You said you'd call him. You told him to get over here."

"You have an exaggerated view of my abilities," Ruben told him. "Well, maybe not all of them. Just the ones involving missing coffee scientists."

"Mm." Victor slid a hand over Ruben's thigh and caressed his quiescent cock. "So we can see Valentin tomorrow, huh?"

Ruben batted at his hand. "You can't grope me while you're talking about another guy!"

Victor laughed. "I'm not interested in any other guy."

"Good. Marc would kill you." Ruben grabbed Victor's wrist and pulled him closer, their bodies fitting together. Only when Victor lay quiet in his arms did Ruben return to their conversation. "Yeah, we can see Valentin tomorrow. He's a lucky bastard, having Marc..." He thought back to the meeting they'd had in the basement of the city archives, with Marc adamant that Valentin had done nothing wrong in reporting his misgivings about the genetically altered coffee.

"He has betrayed no one," Marc had said passionately. "He did a dangerous job and now he pays the price, but I do not consider it a betrayal. Yes, I was angry when he left—but he did it to spare me the wrath of your father, Elias. I came here as soon as I heard on the wire that there was a problem with his flight... and when I heard you'd been arrested in Finland, of all places, I knew there was something very strange going on."

The angel with the startling blue eyes had interrupted. "Mr. Soto asked me to investigate as a personal favor. I found that the aeroplane Mr. Tristan travelled on had landed in Tangiers and changed its flight tags before it continued on to Barcelona."

Marc had placed a paternal hand on the young man's shoulder. "Sebastian has been of great assistance. I'm sure he'll go a long way in the service."

Ruben shook himself from his thoughts. "Yeah," he said with a yawn, "tomorrow we get to see Valentin. I'm sure he and Marc have a lot to talk about tonight. That Sebastian kid was pretty cool, disobeying the general orders from my father to go poking around like he did. Finding the safe house where they were keeping Valentin was good work, especially as he did it in his lunch hour."

Victor nudged against him. "Good to know some angels actually work hard for a living."

"Are you complaining about my playboy lifestyle, buttercup?"

"Not a complaint. Just a comment." Victor's tail curled over and hooked the sheets before pulling up the heavy cotton to cover their bodies. He gave a sleepy sigh. "G'night, Elias. I love you."

Ruben pressed a kiss to his damp hair. "Night, buttercup." He paused, in an agony as to how he should respond, but by the time he plucked up the courage to whisper "I love you, too," Victor was asleep.

* * *

Bright light woke him. Ruben exclaimed, shielding his eyes from the glare. Part of his mind registered that the halogen spotlights installed in the cabin all seemed to be on the highest setting and pointed straight at him. The other part of his mind, the more primal part, registered a scent so familiar it made him feel sick. The smell suffocated him, creeping around him like dark tendrils, rendering him weak and helpless before even a word was said.

Ruben gritted his teeth and rolled off the bed to escape the painful brilliance of the lights. Naked and angry, he faced his father. "Papa, what the fuck?"

Barbosa Major didn't even glance in his direction. His exquisitely tailored suit was immaculate, his hair carefully styled, his gold jewelry discreet yet classy. Everything about him screamed wealth and power, and Ruben loathed him for it—loathed his father for his looks, his magic, and most of all, for his ability to ruin every situation he touched.

"Papa!" Ruben snapped.

But Barbosa ignored him. His attention was solely on Victor, who shrank beneath the sheets and passed a hand through his hair with frantic haste, trying to hide his horns.

"Well, well. My son has been playing with a little demon." Barbosa's crow-black wings fluttered as he dragged the sheets off the bed. He stared at Victor's naked body with a cold, dispassionate expression. "Very nice. You're much prettier than your father."

"What do you know about my father?" Despite being at a marked disadvantage, Victor met Barbosa's stare and lifted his chin in defiance.

"Everything." Barbosa smiled, and it was a chilling sight even for Ruben. "I know he's the Monaco Resident. I know he sent you here to find that pathetic human Valentin Tristan. I know how your father planned the whole operation."

Victor sat up straight, grabbing back the sheet and covering himself with it, his hands bunched tight around the cotton. "How do you know?"

Barbosa laughed. "You think the DTM are the only ones who can pick up transmissions? Dear boy, your silly demon encryptions are no match for a mind as sharp as mine. Tell your father—if you see him again, which is unlikely—it was very foolish of him to let Tristan use the same transmission route all these years. After a while it does tend to arouse suspicion, and when I get suspicious—as my darling son and heir has no doubt told you—I start digging until I find answers."

"You set me up." Ruben heard the words emerge from his throat, snarled and so tight he almost didn't recognize his own voice. "You knew I was accompanying Valentin's plane. Marc asked me to watch over it, to make sure Valentin reached Spain safely!"

"I needed you to witness the crash." Barbosa

finally turned and faced Ruben, who tried not to flinch from the look of spiked dislike in his father's eyes. "I won't pretend I didn't enjoy what I did. After your disgraceful behaviour these past few years—disobeying me, wanting to work in the coffee business like a mere commoner, flaunting your sexuality and your body and your endless stream of lovers—what father could bear to see such waste? Such disgusting profligate brazenness?"

"You didn't care what I did!"

"I cared. I cared very much. It was my name you were dragging through the mud, you depraved creature!" Barbosa's rigid control cracked and his voice rose to a shout. He stepped towards Ruben, lifting his hand, then stopped. He took a deep breath, visibly struggling with his anger, then continued in a shaking voice, "I wanted to give you another chance. A new start. I knew I had to take the opportunity when it was handed to me. I would cut off your wings and make you ugly—and you are ugly, Ruben, so very plain and hopeless without your beautiful wings—and you would help me divert DTM attention away from Tristan."

"Ugly...?" Pain splintered through him, bringing every moment of vulnerability to the surface. Ruben gasped as his heart clenched, but he fought back, rallying his confidence no matter how thin and fake it felt. "I'm not ugly. I'm not hopeless. Victor and I, we worked out what you were doing. We uncovered your plan. And Valentin is safe—Marc is here!" A sudden horrified thought crossed his mind and Ruben caught his breath. "Shit. Marc—did he tell you where we were?"

Barbosa stared at him with a frown. "Marc Soto is in Barcelona? But that's against orders. I'll have him suspended from his post, effective immediately."

Ruben didn't bother to hide his relief. "Then how..."

"One of your crew contacted me." Barbosa's lips twitched into a sneer. "You really are hopeless, son. You go through life blithely trusting everyone and everything. Your wealth may buy you a certain measure of loyalty, but I'm the one with all the power."

"I would rather have loyalty than power," Ruben croaked, angry tears guttering his sight. He blinked, determined not to give his father the satisfaction of seeing him cry. "I would rather have only one loyal friend than all of your toadying, boot-licking minions who secretly despise you!"

Barbosa sighed. "You're such a child. When will you learn that the only loyalty worth having is bought by fear? I would rather have minions than friends, especially if by 'friend' you mean a demon." He cast a contemptuous glance at Victor. "If that's the best you can do, you've sunk lower than I could ever have imagined."

"Victor is worth a hundred of you," Ruben shouted. "A hundred—no, a thousand. Ten thousand!" The words choked in his throat, a sob forming around them. "I hate you. You took my wings. You took everything. I hate you."

Unmoved by Ruben's furious misery, Barbosa raised his eyebrows and arranged his face into an exaggeration of sadness. "Oh, my little boy is unhappy. Perhaps Papa can make you smile again. I'll give you back your wings."

He flicked both hands outwards, delivering a spell-cast. Ruben couldn't block it, had no way to avoid it. He yelped when the magic struck him, a fizz of energy running over his body like the feet and fangs of a thousand biting insects. He tried to scrape it off, but the spell sank into his skin.

"Elias!" Victor shouted. "Elias, are you—"

Ruben tried to reach the bed, but a wave of agony crashed over him, driving him to his knees at his father's feet. Flashes of hot and cold racked his body; sweat rolled from him, the scent of his terror sharp and nauseating. His skin felt too tight, too stretched. His head spun, his vision darkening and bubbling. Tears ran down his face, splashing onto the cabin floor, staining his father's hand-tooled gloss leather shoes.

Dimly, as if from a great distance, Ruben heard Victor's panic-stricken voice calling to him. Ruben shook his head and almost passed out. He tried to push himself upright, but as soon as he got to his knees, fresh pain scraped through him. Whatever his father had done to him, it was unnatural.

White-hot fire seemed to consume him. From his shoulder blades two wings sprouted, slicing free of his body and scattering scraps of flesh and fragments of bone. Ruben collapsed to the floor and screamed. His wings weren't supposed to regenerate like this—they should grow gently over a number of days, but instead it was happening too fast, the bones cracking as his wings opened and flexed, feathers drifting around the cabin as he underwent a dozen moults.

Ruben wished he could faint and escape the pain, but he remained conscious. His wings flapped, brushing against his father's suit, smearing the cloth with streaks of blood and regenerative fluid. Barbosa took a step back with a shudder of disgust, and somehow this hurt more than the physical pain.

"Stop! Please, stop it!" Victor threw back the sheet and dropped to the floor to cradle Ruben in his arms. He didn't flinch from the wings and the blood and slime. He didn't seem to notice it, but bent over Ruben and laid a hand on his forehead. "Elias, tell me what to do. Tell me how to help you—let me share it, let me take some of the pain away..."

Ruben felt the warmth of Victor's touch, felt the gentle spiral of faint, soothing demon magic, but knew Victor couldn't hope to match his father's power. The pain was too all-encompassing for him to speak coherently, so he just stared up and brushed his fingers over Victor's face, trying to smile in reassurance.

"I don't think my son is hurting enough, do you?" Barbosa said conversationally. "Since you want to share his pain, little Bischoff, allow me to assist you in getting your wish." He grabbed Victor's tail and yanked it hard, making him gasp in pain. "This is a very charming tail. I wonder if you would look quite so pretty without it." From his inside jacket pocket Barbosa drew a switchblade, flicking the catch to reveal the glittering steel knife.

Ruben pulled Victor down and kicked at his father's shin, hoping to distract him. Victor struggled, whipping his tail free when Barbosa released him. Victor jumped to his feet and backed into the far wall, his expression wary, his body tensed. Ruben shoved himself upright, though it cost him everything to do so, and blocked his father's path to Victor.

The cabin was too cramped. Ruben curled his wings to give himself more room, but the pain lashed at him again. Unbalanced, he stumbled sideways. Barbosa made his move, shoving Ruben out of his way. Ruben retaliated, striking out at him without thought. He felt the punch connect—I hit my father—and Barbosa grunted as he staggered back. The knife wavered, then Barbosa righted himself and, furious, lunged at Victor, slashing with the blade.

Victor darted to one side but wasn't fast enough. He gave a shocked cry as Barbosa sliced open a shallow cut over his shoulder.

"No," Ruben shouted, transfixed by the thin

trickle of blood down Victor's naked chest. "Victor! Get out of here!"

Barbosa laughed, his breathing short and harsh as he sidestepped across the cabin to block the door. He hefted the knife and beckoned to Victor. "Think you can get past me, boy? Come on, then. Try it. I'll cut off your tail, little demon, and send it to your father."

Victor growled and launched himself at Barbosa, grappling for control of the blade. Ruben held his breath, urging Victor on. For a moment it looked as if the demon would win, but then Barbosa changed his stance. Startled, Victor struggled to regain his balance. The distraction was enough for Barbosa to seize Victor's tail again.

"No!" Ruben lifted his wings, fighting against the blackness that spun around him and the agony flaring with each movement he made. Gathering all his limited magic and the last of his strength, he summoned his rage and blasted it at his father.

Barbosa was hurled out of the cabin, the door falling off its hinges when he struck it. Panting and shaking, Ruben grabbed Victor's hand and leaned against him as they ventured out onto the deck. His cowardly crew had made themselves scarce, leaving the fishing nets spread out on the flat deck of the stern. Barbosa had landed on top of the nets and struggled to free himself of the grasping ropes as he sat up. He kicked at the nets and tossed aside a couple of octopus pots, the ceramic smashing on the wooden deck-boards and skittering against the hull.

His face purple with fury, Barbosa heaved himself to his feet, his black wings flapping. "You've gone too far, boy. I was willing to give you a chance, but you've rejected it. Rejected me. This is where it ends, Ruben. You will renounce your repulsive lifestyle and come home with me now, or you will endure the consequences."

Ruben glared at him. "Fuck you, Papa."

Barbosa gave a laugh of disbelief. "You still reject me—and for him?" He jabbed a finger at Victor. "Is this what you choose—a demon rather than your own flesh and blood?"

"I love him," Ruben said, and heard Victor gasp. "I love him and I want to be with him forever."

Barbosa stared, his expression utterly incredulous. Then he shook himself and raised his arms, hands outstretched. "If you reject me, then you reject everything I gave you. I take back the gift of your wings."

Ruben doubled over as another surge of power brought him to his knees. It felt like his wings were unravelling, the feathers torn out and falling in a white and blue-black storm around him, the delicate bones snapping and splintering, rotting and dying in front of his horrified gaze.

"Stop it!" Victor yelled, hurling himself across the deck at Barbosa. "You evil bastard, stop hurting him!

How can you do this? He's your son!"

Afraid for his lover's safety, Ruben crawled to the external wall of the cabin and used it to push himself upright. He grasped one of the discarded octopus pots as a weapon. "Victor, get back, get—" Ruben stopped, shock freezing the words in his throat as he saw something writhe and twist beneath Victor's skin. As he stared, Ruben saw the flesh strain and give way, tearing open across Victor's back. A pair of demon wings unfurled, glistening wet in the sunlight.

Stunned, Ruben croaked, "Victor!"

"Elias?" Victor turned, anxious concern on his face. He seemed oblivious to his rapidly growing wings, his focus solely on Ruben's safety.

Ruben stared, unable to find the words.

Victor spun full circle, his wings unfolding with a sharp cracking sound. The look of shocked disbelief on Victor's face would have made Ruben laugh under any other circumstances, but now it seemed like the worst kind of irony.

Victor turned back, confused and delighted both at once. He opened his wings, ash-white and glimmering with silver streaks through the translucent webbing. The light caught on them, almost dazzling. For a moment Victor stood lost in awe, staring at his wings, and didn't see the danger.

Ruben yelled a warning just as his father retrieved

the knife from the deck and threw himself at Victor. The knife thrust up then arced down, slashing at Victor's right wing, cutting a rip about ten inches long in the newly-fledged webbing.

Victor howled in furious pain, his wings hunching together as he backed away from Barbosa and the bloodied knife. Ruben ran to him, desperate to save Victor from Barbosa's next strike. Victor's wings were unwieldy, his movements clumsy. Ruben ducked beneath the injured wing and hurled the octopus pot at his father, aiming to knock the knife from his hand.

The pot went wide, glancing off Barbosa's arm and slowing his lunge for only a split-second before he struck again.

"Down!" Ruben shouted, and Victor folded his wings flat. Together they dropped and turned, avoiding Barbosa's wild attack. The trailing edge of Victor's injured wing caught Barbosa, knocking him clear across the deck. Barbosa skidded, his feet tangling in the fishing nets. Unable to regain his balance, he flailed, his wings unfurling and beating as he tried to right himself.

"Papa!" Shaking off Victor's grip, Ruben launched himself at the side of the boat, reaching out to grab his father's crow-black wings.

He was too late. Barbosa fell overboard and hit the water with a huge splash. The nets whizzed over the deck, the weights dropping into the sea with a series of smaller splashes.

Ruben and Victor rushed to the side and looked over. Barbosa struggled briefly, his wings twisted up in the fishing nets, before he sank beneath the surface, leaving a trail of silvery bubbles to mark his passing.

Silence surrounded them. Ruben withdrew his outstretched hand, looking at it as if it didn't belong to him. He could barely comprehend what had just happened. As he stared at the face of the water, his emotions knotted up and tangled round, guilt mixing with relief, grief mingled with happiness.

Victor crept closer and put his arms around Ruben, then after a moment wrapped his wings around him, too. They knelt together in the embrace for a long time, watching the surface of the sea, but Barbosa did not rise again.

EPILOGUE

"Well now, Ruben Patrick, you're a very rich young man." Anton Rasmussen, the Director-General of the FIA, beamed at him across the table, his starling wings telegraphing smug pleasure. "It seems your late father didn't leave a will, so according to Brazilian FIA laws, his wealth will automatically pass to you as his oldest son and heir."

Ruben nodded, still feeling numb after the events of the last few days. He couldn't believe his father was gone; couldn't believe Barbosa's poison would never touch him again. He glanced without interest at the heavy, cream-coloured embossed paper detailing the billions he now held in cash and assets. He didn't want his father's money. Even after giving an equal share to his younger siblings, it would still be too much. "I'm only interested in the coffee plantations."

Anton gave him another unctuous smile. "Of course. That is why Mr. Madsen and I are here, to discuss a strategy for delivering top quality coffee to the DTM. Our old trade agreement had its problems, but from what Marc and Mr. Valdemar Bischoff tell me, it will be a simple and straightforward matter to draw up a new one."

It seemed safest to nod again. Ruben fidgeted, the movement rubbing his back against the chair and reminding him painfully of his wing stumps. They'd ached constantly since he'd lost his wings for a second time. Maybe another glass of red wine would take the edge off it. He lifted his glass, but didn't drink from it. Instead, he looked around the table.

The restaurant in Barri Gotic was closed to all patrons but their little party by order of the FIA. Outside an honor guard stood at attention, snapping at tourists who paused to gawk through the windows. Lined up against a wall as if awaiting a firing squad, a gaggle of serving staff stood ready for orders.

On the opposite side of the circular table was Marc, who sat close to Valentin, one peregrine wing lightly touching the human's shoulder in a protective gesture. Beside Valentin was the Director-General of the DTM, grey-winged Dominik Madsen, who was reading through a pile of papers and highlighting sections of text. Anton Rasmussen met Ruben's gaze, still smiling; Ruben turned his head, repressing a shudder of distaste for the short Frenchman, and looked at Valdemar, who gave Ruben a questioning glance. Unsure of what kind of answer he should give, Ruben dropped his gaze and stared down at where his fingers were entwined with Victor's. He moved his chair closer to his lover and felt the caress of Victor's wings against the nape of his neck. Feeling more confident, Ruben looked back at Anton. "I want this to be a fair agreement."

"Naturally." Anton's smile stretched even wider.

Ruben had thought about this a lot, had talked it through with Victor over the past couple of nights until he was certain of what he wanted. He took a deep breath. "I know the position I'm in. Coffee is the one commodity that could bring angels and demons together, and while I'm not going to hold anyone to ransom politically speaking, as the major shareholder of the world's coffee crop, I am going to insist on transparency in our dealings with one another."

Anton's smile slipped and he began to look worried.

Ruben continued, "I think the divisions between angel and demon are not as great as we've been indoctrinated to believe. Because of this, I intend to spend six months of the year in the DTM with Victor, and Victor will spend six months with me in the FIA. I'm asking you to consider relaxing the border controls to allow free transit between our federated countries—not just for myself and Victor, but for all our citizens. In return for this consideration, Marc and I are willing to negotiate a deal with the FIA government as regards coffee tax benefits, and we're willing to listen to the proposals set forth by the DTM."

Anton's expression had lit up at the words 'tax benefits' and now he nodded, his face wreathed in smiles of approval.

"Coffee is exceedingly important to the DTM," Dominik said. "There are dangers inherent in its consumption, though I believe Valdemar mentioned something about genetic manipulation... something about developing a blend of coffee that produces a high impact effect? Now if we could share the resources that went into the creation of that blend, we'd be able to make a coffee that's pleasing to demons yet without the dangerous side-effects."

Ruben met his gaze. "The resource is me. I blended that coffee."

Anton spoke up quickly, disquiet registering in his voice. "Ruben Patrick, we couldn't possibly expect you to work..."

"Why not? I'm happy to share my knowledge. Valentin can help me, too. There's no one better amongst the human coffee scientists. Between us, we can blend something that's palatable to angels, demons, and humans."

"That's very generous." Dominik pulled out a pocket calculator and tapped away on it for a moment. He nudged Anton. "This is the kind of profit we're looking at, based on those tax margins I showed you earlier. I think it's in our best interests to work together on this one."

Anton blinked at the calculator screen and whistled under his breath. "Oh, yes. All things under Heaven are equal, after all, so I don't see why we can't form a mutually profitable partnership."

Ruben remembered the glass in his hand and took a gulp of wine. He felt the gentle pressure of Victor's wing stroking over his shoulder and smiled gratefully at his lover. Thank God Victor had coached him on what to say at this meeting. There was no way he'd have remembered all that politicizing crap otherwise. He lifted the glass again, inhaling the notes of the wine, but soon put it down, caught by a tendril of Victor's scent. Honeysuckle and sea grass, olive oil on old gold and the first frost of autumn. Ruben gazed at him until Victor dipped his head, his wings of blond hair swinging forward to hide his blush.

Pushing back his chair, Ruben stood, tugging Victor to his feet. He nodded around the table. "Excuse us, gentlemen. We'll be back later."

They walked out of the restaurant hand in hand, past the startled honor guards, and crossed from the shadow of the buildings behind them to the sunlit side of the square closest to the cathedral. They paused by a crumbling old wall the colour of strained honey and stood looking at each other.

"Hey." Victor squeezed his fingers. "How do you feel?"

"Like I want to get back to work." Ruben gave a

short laugh. "Do you think this can happen? A free trade agreement between the FIA and DTM? No more paranoia between angels and demons?"

"I think we can try to make it happen." Victor moved closer and folded his wings, the rip in his right wing a permanent reminder of what they'd both experienced. "Nothing ever changes overnight, but if we have faith..."

"Yeah. If I can reform, anything's possible," Ruben tried to joke.

Victor smiled and took the familiar white and black feather from his jeans pocket. "What's possible is that you'll get your wings back—for real this time. We don't need your father to spell-cast them. With the Director-General's permission and the DNA from this feather, you could have your wings restored to their former glory by the end of the week."

Ruben nodded. "I guess. Somehow it doesn't seem that important. I mean, you have your wings now and—well..."

A slight frown pulled Victor's brows together and he tilted his head. "You don't want to chase my tail through the skies?"

"No. I mean, I do—but..." Ruben freed his hand from Victor's grasp, feeling stupid and inadequate. His father's words rose to echo in his head, and he pushed them back, determined not to fail this time. He wanted Victor to know how he felt without resorting to silly jokes and puerile flirtations. "What I'm trying to say is—you never saw me as something ugly and broken. You never thought I was any less of an angel because I didn't have my wings. So... maybe I don't need them."

Victor gazed at him. "I love you, Ruben Patrick Barbosa."

"Right back at you." Ruben shook off his serious mood and put a hand on Victor's chest, feeling the shape and warmth of his body beneath the shirt. "I wanted to leave the restaurant not because the political stuff was boring—which it was, by the way—but because I wanted to kiss you."

"You can kiss me." Victor leaned against him. "And if you ever change your mind about your wings, I heard about this crazy spell we could try. Now I'm a second rank demon, it's safe for me to have sex with you on a ley line..."

"I don't think so," Ruben said, curling an arm around Victor's waist and holding him close. "I'm not going to risk losing you again—not even for my wings. And as for sex magick... just name the time and place and I'll be there."

"Forever?" Victor asked, a teasing grin lighting his face.

Ruben kissed him. "Forever, buttercup."

ABOUT THE AUTHOR

G. L. Burn is an up-and-coming, British romance author, lover of tea, ruined abbeys, winter, mystery plays, baking, Italy, Yorkshire Terriers, Malta, sea urchins, glaciers, abseiling and archaeology

19601633R00150

Printed in Great Britain
by Amazon